PENGUIN CLASSICS

Maigret and the Lazy Burgl

'Extraordinary masterpieces of the twentieth century'
– John Banville

'A brilliant writer' – India Knight

'Intense atmosphere and resonant detail . . . make Simenon's
fiction remarkably like life' – Julian Barnes

'A truly wonderful writer . . . marvellously readable – lucid,
simple, absolutely in tune with the world he creates'
– Muriel Spark

'Few writers have ever conveyed with such a sure touch, the
bleakness of human life' – A. N. Wilson

'Compelling, remorseless, brilliant' – John Gray

'A writer of genius, one whose simplicity of language creates
indelible images that the florid stylists of our own day can
only dream of' – *Daily Mail*

'The mysteries of the human personality are revealed in all
their disconcerting complexity' – Anita Brookner

'One of the greatest writers of our time' – *The Sunday Times*

'I love reading Simenon. He makes me think of Chekhov'
– William Faulkner

'One of the great psychological novelists of this century'
– *Independent*

'The greatest of all, the most genuine novelist we have had
in literature' – André Gide

'Simenon ought to be spoken of in the same breath as
Camus, Beckett and Kafka' – *Independent on Sunday*

GEORGES SIMENON

Maigret and the Lazy Burglar

Translated by HOWARD CURTIS

PENGUIN BOOKS

PENGUIN CLASSICS

UK | USA | Canada | Ireland | Australia
India | New Zealand | South Africa

Penguin Books is part of the Penguin Random House group of companies
whose addresses can be found at global.penguinrandomhouse.com.

First published in French as *Maigret et le voleur paresseux* by Presses de la Cité 1961
This translation first published 2018
003

Set in 12.5/15 pt Dante MT Std
Typeset by Jouve (UK), Milton Keynes
Printed and bound in Great Britain by Clays Ltd, Elcograf S.p.A.

ISBN: 978-0-241-30391-7

Maigret and the Lazy Burglar

1.

There was a noise not far from his head, and Maigret, reluctantly, almost fearfully, began to move, one of his arms beating the air outside the sheets. He was aware that he was in his bed, aware, too, of the presence of his wife, who, wider awake than he was, was waiting in the darkness without daring to say a word.

What he was mistaken about – at least for a few seconds – was the nature of this insistent, aggressive, imposing noise. And that was a mistake he always made in winter, when it was very cold.

It seemed to him that it was the alarm clock ringing, even though there hadn't been an alarm clock on his bed-side table since he had got married. It all went back even further than his adolescence: to his childhood, in fact, when he had been an altar boy and had served at the six o'clock mass.

And yet he had served at the same mass in spring, summer and autumn, too. Why was the memory that remained with him, that automatically came back to him, a memory of darkness, of frost, of numb fingers, of shoes crunching a thin layer of ice on the way to church?

As so often, he knocked over his glass. Madame Maigret lit the bedside lamp just as his hand reached the telephone.

'Yes, this is Maigret . . .'

It was 3.50, and the silence outside was the silence peculiar to the coldest winter nights.

'Fumel here, detective chief inspector . . .'

'What was that?'

He couldn't hear well. It was as if the person at the other end were talking through a handkerchief.

'Fumel, from the sixteenth . . .'

The man was muffling his voice as if afraid to be heard by someone in an adjoining room. As Maigret did not react, he added:

'Aristide.'

Aristide Fumel, right! Maigret was awake now and wondering why on earth Inspector Fumel from the sixteenth arrondissement was waking him at four in the morning.

And why, in addition, did his voice sound so mysterious, almost furtive?

'I don't know if I did the right thing calling you. I immediately informed my direct superior, the local chief inspector. He told me to call the prosecutor's office. I was put through to the deputy prosecutor on duty.'

Madame Maigret, even though she could only hear her husband's replies, was already getting up, searching for her slippers with her toes, wrapping herself in her quilted dressing gown and heading for the kitchen, where the hissing of the gas was soon heard, followed by water running into the kettle.

'Nobody's quite sure what to do. The deputy ordered me to go back to the scene and wait for him. I wasn't the one who found the body, it was two officers on bicycles.'

'Where?'

'What?'

'I asked you, where?'

'In the Bois de Boulogne. Route des Poteaux. Do you know it? It leads to Avenue Fortunée, not far from Porte Dauphine . . . He's a middle-aged man. More or less my age. As far as I can see, he doesn't have anything in his pockets, no papers. Of course I haven't moved the body. I don't know why, but I get the feeling there's something strange about it and that's why I chose to phone you. It's best if the people from the prosecutor's office don't find out.'

'Thanks, Fumel.'

'I'm going straight back there, in case they get there faster than they usually do.'

'Where are you?'

'At the police station in Rue de la Faisanderie. Are you thinking of coming?'

Maigret hesitated, still buried in the warmth of his bed.

'Yes.'

'What will you say?'

'I don't know yet. I'll think of something.'

He was humiliated, almost furious. Not that this was the first time in the last six months. It wasn't good old Fumel's fault.

'Wrap up warm,' Madame Maigret advised him, from the doorway. 'It's freezing out there.'

Drawing back the curtains, he discovered flowers of frost on the windowpanes. The streetlamps had a special kind of glow that was only seen when it was very cold. There wasn't a soul about on Boulevard Richard-Lenoir, there was no noise, and only one lighted window opposite, presumably in a sickroom.

So now they were being forced to lie! All because of the prosecutor's office, the people from the Ministry of the Interior, all these new lawmakers with their elite education, who had got it into their heads to organize the world according to their own ideas.

As far as they were concerned, the police were merely a cog – a lowly, somewhat shameful cog – in the machine of Justice with a capital J. They weren't to be trusted, had to be closely supervised, given only a subordinate role.

Fumel was still part of the old order, as were Janvier and Lucas and about twenty of Maigret's colleagues, but the others were getting used to the new methods and the new rules, concerned only with preparing for exams in order to rise more quickly through the ranks.

Poor Fumel! He had never been able to rise through the ranks, because he could never learn to spell or write a report!

The prosecutor, or one of his deputies, now had to be the first person informed, the first on the scene, in the company of an examining magistrate who hadn't quite woken up, and these gentlemen gave their opinions as if they had spent their lives discovering bodies and knew more about criminals than anyone else.

As for the police, they were issued with letters of request.

'Do this and that. Apprehend such and such a person and bring him to my office. But whatever you do, don't ask him any questions! Everything has to be done according to the rules . . .'

There were so many rules, the *Official Journal* published so many decrees, often contradictory, that they themselves couldn't make sense of them and lived in fear of being caught out and giving the lawyers an excuse to object.

Sullenly, he got dressed. Why, whenever he was woken on a winter night like this, did the coffee have a particular taste? The smell of the apartment was different, too, reminding him of his parents' house when he woke up at 5.30 in the morning.

'Are you going to phone the office to send you a car?'

No! If he arrived there in a police car, he might be asked to explain himself.

'Phone the taxi rank . . .'

They wouldn't reimburse him for the ride, unless – if this turned out to be murder – he tracked down the killer within a very short time. These days, they only reimbursed taxi fares if you got results. And you still had to prove that you wouldn't have been able to get there any other way.

His wife handed him a thick woollen scarf.

'Do you have your gloves?'

He searched in the pockets of his overcoat.

'Don't you want a bite to eat?'

He wasn't hungry. He seemed to be sulking, and yet, deep down, these were the times he liked, perhaps those he would miss the most when he retired.

He went downstairs and found a taxi waiting for him at the door, white fumes emerging from the exhaust pipe.

'Bois de Boulogne. Do you know the Route des Poteaux?'

'It'd be a bad thing if I didn't know it after thirty-five years in this job.'

This was how veterans consoled themselves for getting older.

The seats were icy. There were only a few cars on the streets, a few empty buses heading for the termini. The first bars hadn't yet opened. On the Champs-Élysées, cleaning women were busy in the offices.

'Another girl who's got herself killed?'

'I don't know. I don't think so.'

'I was thinking she wouldn't have found many clients in the Bois de Boulogne on a night like this.'

His pipe, too, had a different taste. Burying his hands in his pockets, he calculated that he hadn't seen Fumel for at least three months, and that he had known him since . . . pretty much since he himself had first joined the police and was working in a local station.

Fumel was already ugly then, and people already felt sorry for him, while at the same time making fun of him, firstly because his parents had had the idea of calling him Aristide, and secondly because, in spite of his appearance, he was always getting into amorous tangles.

He had got married, and after a year his wife had left him without leaving a forwarding address. He had moved heaven and earth to trace her. For years, a description of her had been in the pocket of every policeman and gendarme in France, and Fumel would rush to the morgue every time a female corpse was fished out of the Seine.

It had become legendary.

'I can't get it out of my head that something terrible happened to her and it was all my fault.'

He had one eye that was fixed. It was brighter than the other, almost transparent, which made his gaze unsettling.

'I'll always love her. And I know I'll find her again one day.'

Did he still hope that, at the age of fifty-one? Not that it prevented him from falling in love periodically. Fate continued to be unkind to him, because all of his affairs were incredibly complicated and ended badly.

He had even, apparently with every justification, been accused of pimping, because of a slut who had played with his affections, and he had narrowly avoided being dismissed from the police force.

Naive and incompetent as he was in his personal life, how did he nevertheless manage to be one of the best inspectors in Paris?

The taxi drove through Porte Dauphine and turned right into the Bois de Boulogne. The light of a torch was already visible. Soon afterwards, shadowy figures could be seen at the side of a path.

Maigret got out of the taxi and paid the fare. One of the figures approached.

'You got here before them,' Fumel sighed, stamping his feet on the icy ground to warm himself.

Two bicycles were leaning against a tree. The officers in their capes were also stamping their feet, while a small man in a pearl-grey bowler hat was impatiently checking the time on his watch.

'Dr Boisrond, from the registry office . . .'

Maigret shook his hand distractedly and walked over to a dark shape at the foot of a tree. Fumel aimed his torch at it.

'I think you'll see what I mean, detective chief inspector,' he said. 'Seems to me there's something not quite right . . .'

'Who found him?'

'Those two officers on bicycles, while they were making their rounds.'

'At what time?'

'Twelve minutes past three. They thought at first it was a bag someone had thrown at the side of the road.'

The man was indeed nothing but a shapeless heap on the ground, in the frost-hardened grass. He wasn't lying full length, but huddled, almost rolled into a ball. One hand stuck out, still clenched, as if he had been trying to grab hold of something.

'What did he die of?' Maigret asked the doctor.

'I hardly dared touch him before the prosecutor's people got here, but as far as I can tell, his skull was fractured by one or several blows with a very heavy object.'

'His skull?' Maigret insisted.

Because by the light of the torch, all he could see of the face was a swollen, bleeding mass of flesh.

'I can't say for certain before the post-mortem, but I'd swear those blows were struck afterwards, when the man was dead, or at least dying.'

'You see what I mean, chief?' Fumel said, looking at Maigret in the semi-darkness.

Without being especially smart, the man's clothes were of good quality, the kind of clothes worn by civil servants or pensioners, for example.

'You say there's nothing in the pockets?'

'I touched them carefully and couldn't feel anything . . . Now look around . . .'

Fumel shone his torch at the ground around the head. There were no bloodstains.

'He wasn't attacked here. The doctor agrees, because, given his wounds, he would have lost a lot of blood. So he was brought into the woods, probably by car. I'd even say, from the way he's all bunched up, that he was pushed out of the car without the people transporting him bothering to get out.'

The Bois de Boulogne was as silent and motionless as a theatre set. Here and there, the streetlights cast well-defined circles of white light.

'Look, I think they're here.'

A long black car was coming from the direction of Porte Dauphine. Fumel waved his torch to light the way and rushed towards the car door.

Maigret, taking small puffs at his pipe, stood aside.

'This way, sir. My chief has had to go to the Hôpital Cochin for a statement. He'll be here in a few minutes . . .'

Maigret had recognized Deputy Prosecutor Kernavel, a tall, thin, well-dressed man in his thirties. He recognized the examining magistrate, too, someone he had rarely had occasion to work with and who in a way straddled the veterans and the new intake, a brown-haired man in his forties named Cajou. As for the clerk of the court, he kept as far away from the body as possible, as if fearing that the sight of it might make him vomit.

'Who—' the deputy prosecutor began.

Then he noticed Maigret and frowned.

'Sorry. I didn't see you at first. How come you're here?'

Maigret responded with a vague gesture and an equally vague phrase:

'Pure chance . . .'

Not at all pleased, from this point on Kernavel made a show of only addressing Fumel.

'What exactly is this all about?'

'Two bicycle officers on their rounds noticed the body just over an hour ago. I alerted my chief, but as I mentioned, he first had to go to the Hôpital Cochin for an urgent statement and he asked me to inform the prosecutor's office. Immediately after that, I called Dr Boisrond here . . .'

Kernavel looked around for the doctor.

'What have you found, doctor?'

'Fractured skull. Probably multiple fractures.'

'Could it have been an accident? Could he have been knocked down by a car?'

'He was struck several times, first on the head, then on the face, with a blunt instrument.'

'So you're certain it was murder?'

Maigret could have kept silent and let them carry on. But he took a step forwards.

'Maybe we could save time by alerting the specialists from Criminal Records?'

It was again to Fumel that the deputy prosecutor gave his instructions.

'Send one of the officers to phone . . .'

He was pale with cold. Everyone was cold, standing around the motionless body.

'A prowler?'

'He isn't dressed like a prowler, and in this weather, there are hardly any in the woods.'

'Was he robbed?'

'As far as I can see, there's nothing in his pockets.'

'So he was on his way home and got attacked?'

'There's no blood on the ground. Like the doctor, I don't think the murder was committed here.'

'In that case, it was probably a gangland killing.'

Kernavel was categorical, pleased to have found a solution appropriate to the problem.

'The murder was probably committed in Montmartre, and the perpetrators brought the body here to get rid of it.'

He turned to Maigret.

'I don't think, inspector, that this is a case for you. I'm sure you have a number of important investigations in progress. Talking of which, how far have you got with the post office hold-up in the thirteenth?'

'Nowhere yet.'

'What about the previous hold-ups? How many have we had, just in Paris, in the last two weeks?'

'Five.'

'That's what I thought. Which is why I'm quite surprised to find you here dealing with an unimportant case.'

It wasn't the first time Maigret had heard this refrain. The gentlemen of the prosecutor's office were alarmed by the latest crime wave, as they called it, and especially by the spectacular robberies which, as periodically happens, had been on the increase recently.

That meant that a new gang had recently formed.

'Still no clues?'

'None at all.'

It wasn't quite true. Although he had no clues, strictly speaking, he nevertheless had a theory that held up and which the facts seemed to confirm. But that was nobody's business, especially not that of the prosecutor's office.

'Listen, Cajou. I want you to deal with this case. If you'll take my advice, make sure it's talked about as little as possible. It's a horrible crime but of no great importance. I mean to say, if these underworld characters start killing each other, it's better for everyone. Do you understand me?'

He turned again to Fumel.

'You're an inspector in the sixteenth, is that right?'

Fumel nodded.

'How long have you been in the police?'

'Thirty years. Twenty-nine, to be exact.'

To Maigret:

'Is he well thought of?'

'He knows his job.'

Kernavel drew the examining magistrate aside and spoke to him in a low voice. When the two men came back, Cajou seemed a little embarrassed.

'Well, detective chief inspector, I thank you for having put yourself out. I'm going to stay in contact with Inspector Fumel here and will give him my instructions. If at any moment I consider that he needs help, I'll issue a letter of request or summon you to my office. You have an important task that requires your urgent attention, so I won't keep you any longer.'

It wasn't just the cold that was making Maigret pale. He gripped his pipe so hard between his teeth that there was a slight cracking of the vulcanite.

'Gentlemen,' he said, as if to take his leave.

'Do you have transport?'

'I'll find a taxi at Porte Dauphine.'

Kernavel hesitated, almost offered to drive him there, but Maigret was already walking away, with a little wave of the hand to Fumel.

Half an hour later, he would probably be able to tell them quite a lot about the dead man. But he wasn't yet sure, which was why he had said nothing.

From the moment he had bent over the body, he had had the impression that he knew who it was. Even though the face had been reduced to a pulp, he would have sworn he had recognized the man.

He only needed one little item of evidence, which they would discover when they stripped the body.

Admittedly, if he was right, they would reach the same conclusion with the fingerprints.

At the taxi rank, he found the same driver who had brought him.

'Finished already?'

'Take me home, to Boulevard Richard-Lenoir.'

'Got it. All the same, it was quick work . . . Who was it?'

A bar was open on Place de la République, and Maigret almost asked the driver to stop, so that he could have a quick drink. Out of a sense of decency, he didn't do so.

Even though his wife had gone back to bed, she heard him climb the stairs and came and opened the door to him. She, too, was surprised.

'So soon?'

Then, immediately afterwards, in an anxious voice:

'What's going on?'

'Nothing. Those gentlemen don't need me.'

He told her as little as he could. It was rare for him to talk about the affairs of Quai des Orfèvres at home.

'Have you eaten anything?'

'No.'

'I'll make you some breakfast. You should have a quick bath to warm yourself up.'

He didn't feel cold any more. His anger had given way to sadness.

He wasn't the only one in the Police Judiciaire to feel discouraged. Even the commissioner had spoken twice of handing in his resignation. He wouldn't have the opportunity to mention it a third time, because they were already talking about replacing him.

They were reorganizing, as they called it. In the silence of their offices, well-educated, well-brought-up young men from the best families in the country were examining all sides of the matter in a quest for greater efficiency. What emerged from their learned cogitations were hare-brained schemes that found expression every week in new rules.

First and foremost, the police had to be a tool at the service of the law. A tool. And a tool, of course, has no brain.

It was the examining magistrate, from his office, and the prosecutor, from his even more prestigious office, who led the investigation and gave the orders.

That wasn't all. To carry out these orders, they didn't want any old-style policemen, those old 'hobnailed boots' who, like Aristide Fumel, couldn't even spell.

When it was mainly now a matter of paperwork, what were they to do with these people who had learned their trade on the beat, tramping the streets, keeping a watch on department stores and railway stations, knowing every bistro in their neighbourhood, every crook, every whore, capable, on occasion, of discussing their jobs with them in their own language?

What was required now was diplomas, exams at every stage of their careers. When he had to arrange a stakeout, Maigret could only count on the few veterans in his team.

They hadn't got rid of him yet. They were waiting, knowing he was only two years from retirement.

Nevertheless, they were starting to supervise everything he did.

It wasn't quite day. As he had his breakfast, more and more lights came on in the windows of the houses opposite. Because of that telephone call, he was ahead of schedule and feeling a little numb, like when you haven't slept enough.

'Is Fumel the one who squints?'

'Yes.'

'The one whose wife left him?'

'Yes.'

'Did they ever find her?'

'They say she got married in South America and has a swarm of children.'

'Does he know?'

'What'd be the point?'

At the office, too, he arrived ahead of time, and, although day had finally broken, he had to light his green-shaded desk lamp.

'Give me the duty office at Rue de la Faisanderie, please.'

He might be barking up the wrong tree. He didn't want to become sentimental.

'Hello? Is Inspector Fumel there? . . . What? He's writing his report?'

More paper, more forms, more wasted time.

'Is that you, Fumel?'

Fumel again spoke in a muffled voice, as if this call had to be kept secret.

'Have Records finished their work?'

'Yes, they left an hour ago.'

'Has the pathologist been on the scene?'

'Yes, the new one.'

Because there was a new pathologist, too. Old Dr Paul, who had still been carrying out post-mortems at the age of seventy-six, had died and been replaced by a man named Lamalle.

'What does he say?'

'He agrees with his colleagues. The man wasn't killed where he was found. He'd lost a lot of blood, there's no doubt about that. The last blows to the face were struck when the victim was already dead.'

'Was the body stripped?'

'Partly.'

'Did you notice a tattoo on the left arm?'

'How did you know about that?'

'A fish? Something like a seahorse?'

'Yes.'

'Did they take fingerprints?'

'They're looking at them right now.'

'Is the body at the Forensic Institute?'

'Yes . . . You know, I was very upset earlier. I still am. But I didn't dare . . .'

'You can already write in your report that, in all probability, the victim is a man named Honoré Cuendet, originally from the Vaud in Switzerland, who once spent five years in the Foreign Legion.'

'The name sounds familiar. Do you know where he lived?'

'No. I know where his mother lives, if she's still alive. I'd prefer to be the first person to talk to her.'

'*They*'ll find out.'

'I don't care. Write down the address, but don't go there before I tell you. It's in Rue Mouffetard. I don't know the number. She's on a mezzanine above a bakery, close to the corner of Rue Saint-Médard.'

'Thanks.'

'Don't mention it. Are you staying in the office?'

'It'll take me another two or three hours to finish this damned report.'

Maigret had not been mistaken, which gave him a certain satisfaction, as well as a touch of sadness. He left his office, climbed the staircase and walked into the fingerprint department, where men in grey smocks were at work.

'Who's handling the prints of the dead man from the Bois de Boulogne?'

'Me, sir.'

'Have you identified him?'

'Just this minute.'

'Cuendet?'

'Yes.'

'Thanks.'

Almost perky now, he walked along other corridors and reached the top floors of the Palais de Justice, where, in Criminal Records, he found his old friend Moers also bent over papers. They had never before accumulated so much paperwork as they had in the past six months. Administrative work had always been important, of course, but Maigret had calculated that, for some time now, it had been taking up about eighty per cent of the time of officers in all departments.

'Did they bring you the clothes?'

'The fellow from the Bois de Boulogne?'

'Yes.'

Moers pointed to two of his colleagues, who were shaking large paper bags in which the dead man's clothes had been sealed. It was routine, the first of the technical procedures. What they had to do was collect dust of all kinds and then analyse it, which sometimes provided them with valuable clues, about the profession of an unknown person, for example, or the place where he usually lived, sometimes about the place where the crime had really been committed.

'What about the pockets?'

'Nothing. No watch, no wallet, no keys. Not even a handkerchief. Absolutely nothing.'

'Any marks on the clothes or underwear?'

'They weren't torn or unstitched. I noted down the name of the tailor. Do you want it?'

'Not now. The man's been identified.'

'Who is he?'

'An old acquaintance of mine, named Cuendet.'

'A criminal?'

'A quiet man, probably the quietest burglar ever.'

'Do you think an accomplice of his did it?'

'Cuendet never had any accomplices.'

'Why was he killed?'

'That's what I'm asking myself.'

Here, too, they were working by artificial light, as was common in offices in Paris these days. The sky was the colour of steel, and out in the streets the road surface was so black that it seemed to be covered with a layer of ice.

People were walking quickly, hugging the buildings, little clouds of steam in front of their faces.

Maigret went back down to the inspectors' room. Two or three were on the telephone; most, of course, were writing.

'Anything new, Lucas?'

'We're still looking for Fernand. Someone thinks they saw him in Paris three weeks ago, but they can't be sure.'

A familiar name. Ten years earlier, this Fernand, whose exact identity had never been established, had been part of a gang that, over a period of a few months, had committed an impressive number of hold-ups.

The whole gang had been arrested, and the trial had lasted nearly two years. The leader had died in prison, of tuberculosis. A few other members were still under lock and key, but the time had come when, having had their sentences reduced for some reason, they were being released one after the other.

Maigret hadn't mentioned this earlier to Deputy Prosecutor Kernavel, in spite of the man's panic at the 'new crime wave'. He had his own ideas on the subject. Certain details of the recent hold-ups had led him to believe that they were the work of old lags who had doubtless formed a new gang.

They just had to find one of them. And to that end, all the men available had been working patiently for nearly three months.

Their search had ended by focusing on Fernand. He had been released a year earlier, but there had been no trace of him for the past six months.

'What about his wife?'

'She still swears she hasn't seen him again. The neighbours confirm that. Nobody's seen Fernand in the neighbourhood.'

'Carry on, boys. If anyone asks for me . . . If anyone from the prosecutor's office asks for me . . .'

He hesitated.

'Tell them I've gone for a drink. Tell them anything . . .'

After all, they couldn't stop him taking an interest in a man he had known for thirty years, a man who had been almost a friend.

2.

He rarely spoke about his job, and even more rarely expressed an opinion about men and their institutions. He distrusted ideas, as they were always too rigid to reflect reality, which, as he knew from experience, was very fluid.

It was only with his friend Pardon, the doctor from Rue Popincourt, that he sometimes, after dinner, came out with what might, at a pinch, pass for revelations.

A few weeks earlier, indeed, he had taken the liberty of speaking with a touch of bitterness.

'People imagine, Pardon, that we're here to track down criminals and obtain their confessions. That's another of those false ideas of which there are so many in circulation and which we get so used to that nobody dreams of examining them. Actually, our main role is to protect the state, first of all, the government, whatever it is, the institutions, then the currency and public property, then the property of individuals, and finally, right at the end, the lives of individuals . . .

'Have you ever been curious enough to look through the penal code? You have to get to page 177 before you find anything about crimes against the individual. Maybe one day, when I'm retired, I'll do a more accurate count, but let's say that three-quarters of the code, perhaps even as much as four-fifths, are about property, counterfeiting, the forging of public or private documents, the poaching of inheritance, and so on and so forth, in other words, everything to do with money. In fact, Article 274, about begging in a public place, comes before Article 295, about voluntary homicide . . .'

And yet they had had a good dinner that night, and had drunk an unforgettable Saint-Émilion.

'In the newspapers, it's my department, the Crime Squad, as everyone calls it, that gets the most attention, because it's the most spectacular. In actual fact, we're less important, in the eyes of the Ministry of the Interior, for example, than Special Branch or the Fraud Squad . . .

'We're a bit like criminal lawyers. We're the public face of things, but it's the civil lawyers who do the serious work, in the shadows.'

Would he have spoken this way twenty years earlier? Or even six months earlier, before these transformations that he had been uneasily witnessing?

He muttered under his breath as, with the collar of his overcoat raised, he crossed Pont Saint-Michel, where the wind was making the pedestrians all bend in the same direction, at the same angle.

He often talked to himself like this, with a grouchy look on his face, and one day he had overheard Lucas saying to Janvier when the latter was still quite new on the team:

'Don't pay any attention. When he's brooding like that, it doesn't necessarily mean he's in a bad mood.'

Or, in fact, that he was unhappy. It was just that something was bothering him. Today, it was the way the men from the prosecutor's office had behaved in the Bois de Boulogne, and the stupid way Honoré Cuendet had met his end: beaten to death, then his face pummelled to a pulp.

'Tell them I've gone for a drink.'

This was the point they had reached. What concerned these highly placed gentlemen was putting an end to the series of hold-ups that were harming the banks and the insurance companies. They were equally bothered by the rise in car thefts.

What if the people collecting the money were better protected? he had objected. What if one man, or two men, weren't entrusted with the task of transporting millions on a route that anybody could find out about?

Too expensive, obviously!

As for the cars, was it normal to leave an object worth a fortune, sometimes the price of a medium-sized apartment or a house in the suburbs, at the kerb, often with the doors unlocked, sometimes even with the key still in the ignition?

You might as well leave a diamond necklace or a wallet containing two or three million francs within reach of whoever came along . . .

What was the point? It was none of his business. He was only a tool, now more than ever, and it wasn't up to him to decide these questions.

All the same, he proceeded to Rue Mouffetard, where, in spite of the cold, he found the usual bustle around the open-air stalls and barrows. Two houses past Rue Saint-Médard, he recognized the narrow bakery with its yellow-painted façade and the low windows of the mez-zanine above it.

The building was old, narrow and high. At the far end of the courtyard, iron could be heard being beaten.

He walked up the stairs, where there was a rope instead of a banister, knocked at a door and soon heard muffled steps.

'Is that you?' a voice asked at the same time as the door-knob turned and the door opened.

The old woman had put on weight, although only from the waist down. Her face was quite thin, her shoulders narrow; her hips, on the other hand, had become enor-mous, so enormous that she walked with difficulty.

She gave him a look full of surprise and anxiety, a look he was accustomed to, common to people who live in fear of misfortune.

'I know you, don't I? You've been here before. Wait . . .'

'Detective Chief Inspector Maigret,' he said, entering a room filled with warmth and the smell of stew.

'That's right, yes. I remember. What are you after him for this time?'

There was no obvious hostility, just a kind of resigna-tion, an acceptance of fate.

She motioned him to a chair. On the worn leather arm-chair, the only one in the apartment, a small ginger dog bared its sharp teeth and gave a low growl, while a cat, white with coffee-coloured patches, half opened its green eyes.

'Be quiet, Toto . . .'

And to Maigret:

'He growls like that, but he's not vicious. He's my son's dog. I don't know if it's because of living with me, but he's ended up looking like me.'

The animal did indeed have a tiny head, a pointed muzzle and thin paws, but a fat body more like a pig's than a dog's. It was probably quite old. Its teeth were yellow and widely spaced.

'Honoré found him in the street about fifteen years ago, with two of his paws crushed by a car. The neighbours wanted the poor animal put down, but Honoré made him a little splint out of pieces of wood, and two months later, he was walking like all the others . . .'

The apartment had a low ceiling and was quite dark but remarkably clean. The room served as both a kitchen and a dining room, with its round table in the middle, its old dresser, its Dutch stove of a kind almost never seen these days.

Cuendet must have bought that stove from the flea market or a junk shop and refurbished it: he had always been good with his hands. The cast iron was almost red, the brasses glowed, and you could hear it humming.

In the street, the market was at its busiest. Maigret recalled that the last time he had been here, he had found the old woman leaning out of the window, which was where she spent most of her time in good weather, looking down at the crowd.

'What can I do for you, inspector?'

She had kept the drawling accent of her native country. Instead of sitting down opposite him, she remained standing, on the defensive.

'When did you last see your son?'

'Tell me first if you've arrested him again.'

He only hesitated for one second and was able to reply without lying:

'No.'

'So you're looking for him? In that case, I can tell you right now he isn't here. You only have to look around the apartment, like you did once before. You won't find anything changed, even though that was more than ten years ago.'

She pointed to an open door, and he glimpsed a dining room that was never used, cluttered with pointless trinkets, table mats and framed photographs: the kind of room you see in the homes of humble people who insist, in spite of everything, on keeping one for show.

Two bedrooms looked out on the courtyard, Maigret knew that: the old lady's room, with an iron bedstead she was determined not to get rid of, and the one that was sometimes occupied by Honoré, which was almost as simple, but more comfortable.

A smell of warm bread rose from the ground floor and mixed with that of the stew.

Maigret was solemn and slightly emotional.

'I'm not looking for him either, Madame Cuendet. I'd just like to know . . .'

Immediately, she seemed to understand, to guess, and her eyes became sharper, with a gleam of anxiety.

'If you're not looking for him and you haven't arrested him, that means . . .'

Her hair was sparsely distributed across a skull that seemed absurdly narrow.

'Something's happened to him, hasn't it?'

He bowed his head.

'I preferred to tell you myself.'

'Did the police shoot him?'

'No. I . . .'

'An accident?'

'Your son is dead, Madame Cuendet.'

She didn't cry, but gave him a harsh look. The ginger dog, which seemed to have understood, jumped down from the armchair and came and rubbed against her fat legs.

'Who did it?'

She hissed these words between teeth as widely spaced as those of the dog, which now started growling again.

'I have no idea. He was killed, we don't yet know where.'

'So how can you say . . .'

'His body was found this morning on a path in the Bois de Boulogne.'

She repeated, suspiciously, as if still sensing a trap:

'The Bois de Boulogne? What would he have been doing in the Bois de Boulogne?'

'That's where he was found. He was killed somewhere else, then driven there by car.'

'Why?'

Trying to avoid upsetting her, he replied patiently:

'That's a question we're asking ourselves too.'

How would he have explained his relationship with Cuendet to the examining magistrate, for example? It wasn't only in his office at Quai des Orfèvres that he had got to know him. And it had taken more than just one partly solved case.

It involved thirty years on the job, including several visits to this apartment, which felt familiar to him.

'It's in order to track down his killers that I need to know when you last saw him. He hasn't slept here in several days, has he?'

'At his age, he's entitled . . .'

She broke off, her eyelids suddenly swollen.

'Where is he right now?'

'You'll see him later. An inspector will come and fetch you.'

'Has he been taken to the morgue?'

'To the Forensic Institute, yes.'

'Did he suffer?'

'No.'

'Was he shot?'

Tears were running down her cheeks, but she didn't sob and was still looking at Maigret with a vestige of suspicion.

'He was beaten.'

'With what?'

It was as if she were trying to reconstruct her son's death in her mind.

'We don't know. A heavy object.'

Instinctively, she raised her hand to her head and gave a grimace of pain.

'Why?'

'We'll find out, I swear to you. It's why I'm here and it's why I need you. Please sit down, Madame Cuendet.'

'I can't.'

And yet her knees were shaking.

'Do you have anything to drink?'

'Why, are you thirsty?'

'No. It's for you. I think you should have a little something.'

He remembered that she liked to drink and, indeed, she went and took a bottle of white brandy from the dresser in the dining room.

Even at a time like this, she felt the need to lie a little.

'I was keeping it for my son. He sometimes had a drop after dinner.'

She filled two thick-bottomed glasses.

'I wonder why they killed him,' she repeated. 'A boy who never harmed anyone, the quietest, gentlest man in the world. Isn't that so, Toto? You know that better than anyone.'

As she wept, she stroked the fat dog, which wagged its stunted tail. The scene would doubtless have seemed grotesque to Kernavel and Cajou.

Wasn't that son of hers a known criminal, who might, if he hadn't been so clever, still have been in prison?

He had only gone to prison twice, once merely remanded in custody, and both times it had been Maigret who had arrested him.

They had spent many hours alone together at Quai des Orfèvres, two cunning men with a sense of one another's true worth.

'How long . . .'

Maigret had returned to the task in hand, patiently, in an even voice, with the noises of the market in the background.

'At least a month,' she said, yielding at last.

'Did he tell you anything?'

'He never told me anything about what he did outside of here.'

It was true: Maigret had had proof of that before.

'Did he come to see you even once during this time?'

'No, although it was my birthday last week. He did send me flowers.'

'Where did he send them from?'

'He had them delivered.'

'Was the name of the florist on them?'

'Maybe. I didn't look.'

'Did you recognize the delivery man? Was he local?'

'I'd never seen him before.'

He didn't ask to search Honoré Cuendet's room for clues. He wasn't here officially. He hadn't been entrusted with the investigation.

Inspector Fumel would doubtless come later, equipped with papers duly signed by the examining magistrate. He probably wouldn't find anything. The previous times, Maigret hadn't found anything either, just neatly arranged clothes, underwear in the wardrobe, a few books, tools that weren't a burglar's tools.

'How long is it since he last disappeared like that?'

She searched in her memory. She was no longer fully involved in the conversation and had to make an effort.

'He spent almost all winter here.'

'What about the summer?'

'I don't know where he went.'

'Didn't he offer to take you to the country, or the sea?'

'I wouldn't have gone. I lived long enough in the country not to want to go back.'

She had probably been about fifty, perhaps a little older, when she had discovered Paris. Before that, the only city she had known was Lausanne.

She was from a little village in the canton of Vaud, Senarclens, not far from a town called Cossonay, where her husband, Gilles, worked as a farm labourer.

Maigret had only ever been through the country on holiday with his wife, and what he remembered above all was the inns.

It was these inns, as it happened, clean and quiet, which had been Gilles Cuendet's undoing. A short man with twisted legs, he wasn't a great talker and could spend hours in a corner, drinking bottles of white wine.

He had given up labouring and become a mole catcher, going from farm to farm laying his traps, and it was said that he smelled as strongly as the animals he caught.

They had two children, Honoré and his sister Laurence, who had been sent to Geneva to work as a waitress and ended up marrying someone from UNESCO, a translator, if Maigret's memory was correct, and following him to South America.

'Have you heard from your daughter?'

'I had New Year greetings from her. She has five children now. I can show you the card.'

She went to fetch it from the next room, more out of a need to move than to convince him.

'Look, it's in colour.'

The image showed the port of Rio de Janeiro beneath a purple-red sunset.

'Doesn't she ever write more than that?'

'What's the point? With the ocean between us, we'll never see each other again. She's made her own life, hasn't she?'

Honoré had made his, too, though in quite a different way. At the age of fifteen he, too, had been sent away to work, in his case as an apprentice to a locksmith in Lausanne.

He had been a quiet, reserved young man, hardly more talkative than his father. He had lived in an attic room in an old house near the market, and it was following an anonymous tip-off that the police had burst into that room one morning.

Honoré wasn't yet seventeen at the time. They had found all kinds of things there, the most heterogeneous objects, the provenance of which he hadn't even tried to explain: alarm clocks, tools, canned food, children's clothes still with their labels attached, two or three radio sets that hadn't been taken out of their original packaging.

The police had thought at first that these things had all been stolen from parked vans.

Upon investigation, they had realized that this was not the case, that young Cuendet had broken into closed shops, warehouses and empty apartments and taken at random whatever he could find.

Because of his age, he had been sent to the reformatory at Vennes, above Lausanne, where, among the trades he had been given the chance to learn, he had chosen that of boilermaker.

For a year, he had been a model inmate, quiet and gentle, hard-working, never breaking the rules. Then, suddenly, he had vanished without a trace, and ten years were to go by before he came to Maigret's attention in Paris.

His first concern, on leaving Switzerland, where he had never again set foot, had been to join the Foreign Legion, and he had spent five years first in Sidi-Bel-Abbès, then in Indochina.

Maigret had had occasion to look through his military record and to talk to one of his commanding officers.

There again, Honoré Cuendet had been, generally, a model soldier. The most that could be held against him was that he was a lone wolf, someone who had no friends and didn't mix with the others, even on evenings when they got into brawls.

'He was a soldier the way some people are metalworkers or cobblers,' his lieutenant had said.

No punishment in three years. After which, for no known reason, he had deserted, to be found again, a few days later, in a workshop in Algiers where he had been hired.

He had furnished no explanation for his sudden departure, which could have cost him dearly, merely murmuring:

'I couldn't stand it any more.'

'Why not?'

'I don't know.'

Thanks to his three years of impeccable service, he had

been treated leniently, and six months later he had done it again, this time getting caught after only twenty-four hours of freedom, found in a vegetable lorry where he had been hiding.

It was in the Legion that he had had a fish tattooed on his left arm, at his request, and Maigret had wanted to know why.

'Why a fish?' he had insisted. 'And above all, why a seahorse?'

Legionnaires usually have a taste for more evocative images.

The man Maigret had had in front of him at that time was twenty-six years old, fairly short, with reddish-blond hair and broad shoulders.

'Have you ever seen a seahorse?'

'Not alive.'

'What about dead?'

'I've seen one.'

'Where?'

'In Lausanne.'

'Where in Lausanne?'

'In a woman's bedroom.'

The words had to be dragged from him almost one by one.

'What woman?'

'A woman I went with.'

'Was this before you were sent to Vennes?'

'Yes.'

'Was she on the street?'

'At the end of Rue Centrale, yes.'

'And in her room there was a dried seahorse?'

'That's right. She told me it was her lucky charm.'

'Have you known many other women?'

'Not many.'

Maigret thought he had understood.

'What did you do when you got away from the Legion and came to Paris?'

'I worked.'

'Where?'

'At a locksmith's in Rue de la Roquette.'

The police had checked. It was true. He had been there for two years, and his work had been eminently satisfactory. They made fun of him because he wasn't very talkative, but he was considered a model worker.

'How did you spend your evenings?'

'Doing nothing.'

'Did you ever go to the cinema?'

'Almost never.'

'Did you have any friends?'

'No.'

'What about girlfriends?'

'Definitely not.'

It was as if women scared him. And yet, because of the first one he had known, at the age of sixteen, he had had a seahorse tattooed on his arm.

They had investigated thoroughly. In those days, they could afford to be meticulous. Maigret was only an inspector then, barely three years older than Cuendet.

It happened rather as it had in Lausanne, except that this time there hadn't been any anonymous letter.

Early one morning – about four o'clock, in fact, as with the discovery of the body in the Bois de Boulogne – a uniformed officer had stopped a man carrying a heavy package. It was pure chance. The man's first reaction had been to make as if to run away.

In the package, they had found furs, and Cuendet had refused to explain away this strange burden.

'Where were you going with that?'

'I don't know.'

'Where have you come from?'

'I have nothing to say.'

They finally discovered that the furs belonged to a furrier who worked from home, in Rue des Francs-Bourgeois.

At the time, Cuendet was living in a rooming house in Rue Saint-Antoine, a hundred metres from the Bastille, and in his room, as in the attic in Lausanne, they had found an assortment of the most diverse merchandise.

'Who were you selling your loot to?'

'Nobody.'

It seemed far-fetched, and yet it had been impossible to establish a link between Cuendet and any of the known fences.

He didn't have much money on him. His expenses corresponded with what he earned from his employer.

The case had intrigued Maigret to such an extent that he had obtained permission from his then chief, Commissioner Guillaume, for the prisoner to be examined by a doctor.

'He's certainly what we call an asocial type, but he also has above-average intelligence and normal emotional responses.'

Cuendet had been lucky enough to be defended by a young lawyer, Maître Gambier, who was later to become a leading light of the legal profession and who had obtained the minimum sentence for his client.

Initially incarcerated in the Santé, Cuendet had spent just over a year in Fresnes, where, once again, he had been a model prisoner, which had earned him a few months' remission on his sentence.

In the meantime, his father had died, knocked down by a car one Saturday evening when he was on his way home, drunk, on a bicycle without lights.

Honoré had his mother brought from Senarclens, and this woman who had only known the quietest country-side in Europe had found herself transplanted into the midst of the swarming crowds in Rue Mouffetard.

Wasn't she, too, a kind of phenomenon? Instead of pan-icking and taking a dislike to the big city, she had settled down in her new neighbourhood, in her street, taking root to such an extent that she had become one of the most popular characters there.

Her name was Justine. From one end of Rue Mouffetard to the other, everyone now knew old Justine with her drawling speech and the mischievous gleam in her eyes.

The fact that her son had been in prison didn't embar-rass her in the least.

'Everyone has his own tastes and his own opinions,' she would say.

Maigret had twice more had dealings with Honoré Cuendet, the second time after a major theft of jewellery in Rue de la Pompe, in Passy.

The burglary had taken place in a luxurious apartment where there were three live-in servants in addition to their masters. In the evening, the jewels had been placed on a dressing table in the boudoir next to the bedroom, the door of which had remained open all night.

Neither Monsieur nor Madame D., who had been sleeping in their bed, had heard anything. The chambermaid, who slept on the same floor, was sure she had locked the door to the apartment and had found it still locked in the morning. No sign of forced entry. No fingerprints.

As the apartment was on the third floor, there was no question of someone having climbed up. There was no balcony either, which might have made it possible to reach the boudoir through an adjoining apartment.

It was the fifth or sixth robbery of this kind in three years, and the newspapers were starting to talk of a phantom burglar.

Maigret remembered that spring, remembered how Rue de la Pompe had looked at every hour of the day, because he had gone from door to door, tirelessly questioning people, not only the concierges and the shopkeepers, but the tenants of the apartment buildings and the servants.

That was how – by chance, or rather, out of stubbornness – he had come across Cuendet. In the building opposite the house where the burglary had taken place, a garret looking out on the street had been rented six weeks earlier.

'It's occupied by a very nice, very quiet gentleman,' the concierge said. 'He doesn't go out very much, never goes out in the evening and never has women visitors. In fact, he never has any visitors.'

'Does he do his own cleaning?'

'Of course. And it really is clean, believe me!'

Was Cuendet so sure of himself that he hadn't bothered to move house after the robbery, or had he been afraid he would arouse suspicion if he left?

Maigret had found him at home, reading. By looking out of the window, he had been able to follow all the comings and goings of the tenants in the apartments opposite.

'I must ask you to follow me to police headquarters.'

Cuendet hadn't protested. He had allowed his room to be searched without saying a word. Nothing had been found, no jewels, no skeleton keys, no burglar's tools.

The interrogation at Quai des Orfèvres had lasted nearly twenty-four hours, interspersed with beer and sandwiches.

'Why did you rent that room?'

'Because I liked it.'

'Have you quarrelled with your mother?'

'No.'

'Don't you live with her any more?'

'I'll go back there one of these days.'

'You've left most of your things there.'

'Precisely.'

'Have you been to see her lately?'

'No.'

'Who have you met?'

'The concierge, the neighbours, people passing in the street.'

His accent gave his answers an irony that might have been involuntary, because his face remained calm and serious. He seemed to be doing all he possibly could to satisfy Maigret.

The interrogation had yielded nothing, but the investigation in Rue Mouffetard had provided them with grounds for suspicion. It emerged that this wasn't the first time that Cuendet had disappeared for a while. These absences generally varied from three weeks to two months. After them, he always moved back in with his mother.

'What do you live on?'

'I do odd jobs. I've put a little money aside.'

'In a bank?'

'No. I don't trust banks.'

'Where is this money?'

He wouldn't say. Since his first arrest he had studied the penal code, and now knew it by heart.

'It's not up to me to prove my innocence. It's up to you to establish my guilt.'

Only once had Maigret lost his temper. Faced with Cuendet's air of gentle reprimand, he had immediately regretted it.

'You got rid of the jewels one way or another. It's quite likely you sold them. Who to?'

They had, of course, done the rounds of the known fences and had alerted Antwerp, Amsterdam and London. They had also passed the word to their informers.

Nobody knew Cuendet. Nobody had seen him. Nobody had been in contact with him.

'What did I tell you?' his mother had said triumphantly.

'I know you're clever, but my son, don't you see, is really somebody!'

In spite of his criminal record, in spite of the garret, in spite of everything that pointed to him, they had been obliged to release him.

Cuendet hadn't crowed about it. He had taken the matter calmly. Maigret could still see him, looking for his hat, stopping by the door, reaching out a hesitant hand.

'See you again, inspector.'

As if he expected to be back!

3.

The chairs had seats of woven straw and gleamed golden in the semi-darkness. The floor, although of common fir wood and very old, was so well polished that you could see the rectangle of the window in it as if it were a mirror. The brass pendulum of a clock on the wall swung at a peaceful rhythm.

It was as if the smallest object – the poker, the bowls with their big pink flowers, even the broom against which the cat was rubbing its back – had a life of its own, as if in an old Dutch painting or in a sacristy.

Madame Cuendet opened the stove and put in two shovelfuls of glossy coal. For a moment, the flames licked her face.

'Do you mind if I take off my coat?'

'Does that mean you're going to stay for a long time?'

'It's minus five outside, but in here it's quite hot.'

'They say old people feel the cold more,' she muttered, more to herself, to occupy her mind, than to him. 'In my case, my stove keeps me company. My son was like that, too, even when he was young. I can still see him, in our house in Senarclens, right up against the stove, doing his homework.'

She looked at the empty armchair, the polished wood, the worn leather.

'Here, too, he liked to be close to the fire and could spend days reading without hearing anything.'

'What kind of things did he read?'

She lifted her arms in a gesture of powerlessness.

'How should I know? Books he got from the reading room in Rue Monge. Look, here's the last one. He used to exchange them as he went along. He had a kind of subscription. You must know about that.'

Bound in shiny black canvas, it was a work by Lenotre on an episode of the Revolution.

'He knew a lot of things, my Honoré. He didn't talk a lot, but his mind never stopped working. He read newspapers, too, four or five a day, and big, expensive magazines with colour pictures.'

Maigret liked the smell of the apartment, made up of lots of different smells. He had always had a weakness for dwellings that have a characteristic smell, and he hesitated to light his pipe, which he had filled mechanically.

'You can smoke. He smoked a pipe, too. He was so fond of his old pipes, he'd actually mend them with wire.'

'I'd like to ask you a question, Madame Cuendet.'

'It's funny to hear you call me that. Everybody's been calling me Justine for so long now! I actually think that, apart from the mayor, when he congratulated me the day I got married, nobody has ever called me anything else. But go on. I'll answer you if I feel like it.'

'You don't work. Your husband was poor.'

'Have you ever met a rich mole catcher? Especially a mole catcher who drinks from morning till night?'

'So you live on the money your son gave you.'

'Is there any harm in that?'

'A manual worker gives his pay to his wife or mother every week, an office worker every month. I assume Honoré would give you money as you needed it?'

She looked at him closely, as if grasping the significance of the question.

'What of it?'

'Well, for instance, he might have given you a large sum when he came back after being away.'

'There were never any large sums here. What would I have done with them?'

'These absences of his lasted quite a long time, sometimes weeks, didn't they? If you needed money during that time, what did you do?'

'I didn't need it.'

'So he gave you enough before he left?'

'Not to mention the fact that I have an account with the butcher and the grocer, and that I can buy on credit from any shopkeeper in the neighbourhood and even from the barrow boys. Everyone in the street knows old Justine.'

'Did he ever send you a money order?'

'I don't know how I'd have gone about collecting it.'

'Listen, Madame Cuendet—'

'I'd prefer it if you called me Justine.'

She was still standing. She added a little more hot water to her stew and replaced the lid, leaving a slight gap for the steam.

'I can't cause him any more trouble, and I have no intention of causing you any. What I'm trying to do is find the people who killed him.'

'When will I be able to see him?'

'Probably this afternoon. An inspector will come and fetch you.'

'And will they hand him over to me?'

'I think so. But in order to find his killer, or killers, I need to understand certain things.'

'What do you want to understand?'

She was still suspicious, like the peasant woman she had remained, like an old, barely literate woman who senses traps everywhere. She couldn't help it.

'Your son left you several times a year and was away for several weeks.'

'Sometimes three weeks, sometimes two months.'

'How was he when he came back?'

'Like a man who's pleased to find his slippers by the fire.'

'Did he tell you when he was planning to leave, or did he just go without saying a word?'

'Who do you think packed his suitcase for him?'

'So he did tell you. He took spare clothes with him, underwear . . .'

'He took everything he needed.'

'Did he have several suits?'

'Four or five. He liked to be well dressed.'

'Did you have the impression that when he got back, he hid things in the apartment?'

'It wouldn't be easy to find a hiding place in these four rooms. Besides, you searched them, and more than once. I remember that your men ferreted everywhere and even dismantled the furniture. They went down to the cellar, even though it's common to all the tenants, and up to the corner of the attic that we're allowed to use.'

It was true. They had found nothing.

'Your son didn't have a bank account, we've checked that, or a savings account. But he must have deposited his money somewhere. Do you know if he ever went abroad, to Belgium, for example, or Switzerland, or Spain?'

'In Switzerland, he would have been arrested.'

'That's right.'

'He never talked about the other countries you mentioned.'

Several times, they had alerted the borders. For years, a photograph of Honoré Cuendet had been included among those of people who needed to be looked out for in railway stations and at other exits from the country.

Maigret was thinking aloud.

'He must have sold the jewels and other objects he stole. He didn't use professional fences. And as he didn't spend much money, he must have had a sizeable sum somewhere.'

He was looking more closely at the old lady now.

'If he only gave you housekeeping money as you needed it, what's going to become of you now?'

This idea struck her, and she shuddered. He saw a touch of anxiety in her eyes.

'I'm not afraid,' she nevertheless replied proudly. 'Honoré is a good son.'

She didn't say 'was' this time. And she continued, as if he were still alive:

'I'm sure he won't leave me without anything.'

'He wasn't killed by a prowler,' Maigret resumed, 'and it wasn't a random act. Nor was he shot down by an accomplice.'

She didn't ask him how he knew this, and he didn't explain. A prowler wouldn't have had any reason to disfigure the face or empty the pockets of the slightest objects, including unimportant papers, pipe, matches.

An accomplice wouldn't have done that either, knowing that Cuendet had been in prison and would consequently be identified by his fingerprints.

'The man who killed him didn't know him. And yet he had an important reason to get rid of him. Do you understand?'

'What am I supposed to understand?'

'That when we find out what job Honoré was preparing, and what house or apartment he broke into, we'll be very close to knowing who killed him.'

'It won't bring him back to life.'

'Do you mind if I take a look in his room?'

'I can't stop you.'

'I'd rather you came with me.'

She shrugged and followed him, swaying her almost monstrous hips, and the little ginger dog trotted after them, ready to growl again.

The dining room was neutral, lifeless, almost odourless. The old woman's iron bedstead was covered in a very white counterpane. Honoré's room, poorly lit by a window that looked out on to the yard, was already taking on a funereal appearance.

Maigret opened the door of a mirrored wardrobe, found

three suits on hangers, two of them grey and one navy-blue, shoes lined up at the bottom and, on a shelf, shirts with a bouquet of dried lavender on top of the pile.

On a bookshelf stood a red copy of the penal code, quite worn, which must have been bought down by the river or from a second-hand bookshop on Boulevard Saint-Michel; several novels dating from the beginning of the century, plus a Zola and a Tolstoy; a map of Paris which looked as if it had been much consulted . . .

On a two-level console table in a corner lay magazines whose titles made Maigret frown. They didn't fit with all the rest. They were thick, luxurious magazines on glossy paper, with colour photographs of the most beautiful chateaus in France as well as sumptuous interiors in Paris.

He leafed through some of them, hoping to find notes, pencil marks.

In Lausanne, young Cuendet, an apprentice locksmith living in a garret, had grabbed everything he came across, including objects of no value.

Later, in Rue Saint-Antoine, he was to show a little more discrimination, but still only burgled random local shops and apartments.

Then he climbed another rung, breaking into middle-class houses, where he found both money and jewellery.

At last, patiently, he had reached the ritzier parts of town. Without meaning to, the old woman had said something important earlier. She had mentioned the four or five newspapers her son read every day.

Maigret would have sworn that it wasn't the crime news he sought out, let alone the political news, but the society columns: weddings, accounts of receptions, dress rehearsals.

Wasn't that the place where the jewellery worn by women in the public eye was described?

The magazines that Maigret now had in front of his eyes had also provided Honoré with valuable information: not only meticulous descriptions of mansions and apartments, but even photographs of the different rooms.

Sitting by the fire, Cuendet had pondered, weighed the pros and cons and made his choice.

Then he would go and prowl around the neighbourhood, renting a room in a hotel or, if he could find one, in a private house, as had been the case in Rue de la Pompe.

During the last investigation, which had been several years previously, they had also picked up his trail in a certain number of cafés, where he had suddenly become a regular, for a time at least.

'A very quiet man, who spent hours in his corner, drinking white wine, reading the papers and looking out at the street . . .'

In reality, he had been observing the comings and goings of masters and servants in a house, studying their habits, their timetables. Later, from his own window, he would spy on them as they moved about indoors.

In this way, an entire building would eventually yield up all its secrets to him.

'Thank you, Madame Cuendet.'

'Justine!'

'I'm sorry: Justine. I had a lot of . . .'

He searched for the word. Friendship was too strong.

If he said he felt a fondness for him, she wouldn't understand what he meant.

'I had a lot of respect for your son.'

That wasn't quite the right word either, but neither the
deputy prosecutor nor the examining magistrate was
there to hear him.

'Inspector Fumel will come and see you. If you need
anything, please get in touch with me.'

'I won't need anything.'

'If you should happen to find out where Honoré spent
the last few weeks . . .'

He put on his heavy overcoat and carefully descended
the staircase with its worn steps. He found himself back
in the cold and noise of the street. There was now a little
white powder hanging in the air, as it were, but it wasn't
snowing, and there was no trace of it on the ground.

When he entered the inspectors' room, Lucas announced:

'Moers phoned to ask for you.'

'Did he say why?'

'He'd like you to call him.'

'Still no news of Fernand?'

He had forgotten that his main task was to track down
the gang doing all these hold-ups. It might last weeks,
maybe months. Hundreds, thousands of police officers
and gendarmes had Fernand's photograph in their pockets. Inspectors were going door to door, like vacuum-cleaner
salesmen.

'Sorry to bother you, madame. Have you seen this man
recently?'

Hotel records were checked. The Vice Squad questioned

prostitutes. In the railway stations, travellers had no idea that anonymous eyes were inspecting them as they passed.

The Cuendet murder wasn't his case. He didn't have the right to take his men away from what they were doing. He nevertheless found a way to reconcile his duty and his curiosity.

'Go upstairs and ask for a photograph of Cuendet, the most recent one they have. Have a copy sent to all the men who are looking for Fernand, especially the ones visiting the bistros and the rooming houses.'

'In every neighbourhood?'

He hesitated, and almost replied:

'Only in the wealthy neighbourhoods.'

But then he remembered that mansions and luxury apartment houses can also be found in the older neighbourhoods.

Once in his office, he called Moers.

'Have you found anything?'

'I don't know if this is any use to you. Examining the clothes with a magnifying glass, my men discovered three or four hairs, which they then put under a microscope. Delage, who's an expert on these things, says they're wildcat hairs.'

'What part of the clothes were they on?'

'On the back, near the left shoulder. There are also traces of rice powder. We may be able to determine the brand, but that'll take longer.'

'Thanks. Has Fumel called you?'

'He was just here. I told him what I've told you.'

'Where is he?'

'In Records, engrossed in the Cuendet file.'

Maigret wondered for a moment why his eyes were smarting, then remembered that he had been dragged from his bed at four in the morning.

He had to sign a few papers, fill in a few forms and see two people who had been waiting to speak to him and to whom he listened with half an ear. Once alone, he called a big furrier in Rue La Boétie and had to insist before he was put through to him personally.

'Detective Chief Inspector Maigret, Police Judiciaire. Sorry to bother you, but I'd like some information. Can you tell me roughly how many wildcat fur coats there are in Paris?'

'Wildcat?'

The man seemed annoyed by the question.

'We don't have any here. There was a time, in the early days of automobiles, when we did make them for some of our customers, especially male ones.'

Maigret recalled old photographs of motorists looking like bears.

'That was from wildcat fur?'

'Not always, but the most beautiful ones were. They're still worn in very cold countries, in Canada, Switzerland, Norway and the north of the United States.'

'Are there any in Paris?'

'I think some shops still sell them, but not many. It's not easy to quote a precise figure. I'd be surprised if there were more than five hundred coats like that in the whole of Paris, and most of them must be quite old. These days . . .'

An idea had occurred to him.

'Are you only interested in coats?'

'Why?'

'Because we very occasionally use wildcat for non-clothing purposes. For example, for throws on sofas. They can also be used in cars, as rugs.'

'Are there many of them?'

'Looking in our books, I'd be able to tell you how many have come from here in the last few years. Three or four dozen, I'd guess. But there are furriers who mass-produce them. The quality isn't as good, of course . . . Wait, I just thought of something else. As I was speaking to you, I remembered the window of a pharmacy not far from here, displaying a wildcat skin that was being sold as a cure for rheumatism.'

'Many thanks.'

'Would you like me to draw you up a list of—'

'If it's not too much trouble.'

It was quite discouraging. For weeks, they had been looking for Fernand without any certainty that he was mixed up in the recent hold-ups. It was an amount of work almost as considerable as compiling a dictionary, for example, or even an encyclopedia.

And yet they knew Fernand, his tastes, his habits, his obsessions. There was one quite trivial detail, for example, that might help to track him down: he never drank anything but mandarin curaçaos.

Now, as a possible clue that might lead them to Cuendet's killers, they had a few wildcat hairs.

Moers had said that these hairs had been found on the

back of the jacket, near the left sleeve. If they were from a coat, wouldn't they more likely have been found on the front of the suit?

Had a woman helped to carry him, holding him by the shoulders?

Maigret preferred the hypothesis of a cover, something like a travelling rug. And in that case, it wasn't just any small car: fur rugs were hardly ever used in a 4CV.

Hadn't Cuendet been breaking into rich houses exclusively for the past few years?

They would have to do the rounds of all the garages in Paris, tirelessly asking the same question.

There was a knock at the door. It was Inspector Fumel, red-faced and red-eyed. He had slept even less than Maigret. In fact, having been on duty the previous night, he hadn't slept at all.

'I'm not disturbing you, am I?'

'Come in, old friend.'

There weren't many officers with whom Maigret was so familiar, veterans mainly, men he had started his career with and who had been equally familiar with him but who now no longer dared call him anything but detective chief inspector or, sometimes, just chief. There was Lucas, too. Not Janvier, he didn't know why. And finally the newer ones, like young Lapointe.

'Take a seat.'

'I read everything about him. To be honest, I don't even know where to start. A team of two men wouldn't be enough. I realized, reading the statement transcripts, that you knew him well.'

'Quite well. This morning I went to see his mother, unof-ficially. I broke the news to her and told her that you'd soon be over to see her and take her to the Forensic Institute. Have you heard anything about the results of the post-mortem?'

'Nothing. I phoned Doctor Lamalle. I was told through his assistant that he'd be sending his report to the examin-ing magistrate this evening or tomorrow.'

Doctor Paul had never waited for Maigret to call him. He had sometimes even asked:

'What should I tell the examining magistrate?'

True, in those days, the police had been in charge of the investigation, and most of the time the magistrate only got involved once the guilty party had confessed.

There had been three distinct phases: the investigation, which, in Paris, was the business of Quai des Orfèvres; the examination; and finally, later, after the file had been studied by the prosecutor's office, the trial.

'Did Moers tell you about the hairs?'

'Yes. Wildcat.'

'I've just phoned a furrier. You'd do well to find out about wildcat covers or rugs that have been sold in Paris. Then question the garage owners . . .'

'I'm all on my own.'

'I'm aware of that, my friend.'

'I sent in my preliminary report. Judge Cajou wants to see me at five this afternoon. There's going to be no end of a fuss. As I was on duty last night, I was supposed to have a day off today, and there's someone waiting for me. I'll phone, but I know they won't believe me, and it'll cause all kinds of complications . . .'

A woman, of course!

'If I find anything, I'll phone you. But don't tell the examining magistrate I'm doing it.'

'Understood!'

Maigret went home for lunch. The apartment was as clean, the floors and furniture as well polished, as in old Madame Cuendet's place.

It was hot here, too, and there was a stove, in spite of the radiators, because Maigret had always loved stoves, and for a long time the administration had let him keep one in his office.

There was a lovely, pervasive smell of cooking. And yet it suddenly struck him that something was missing, he couldn't have said what.

In Honoré's mother's apartment, the atmosphere was even calmer and more enveloping, perhaps by contrast with the bustle of the street. Through the window, you could almost touch the stalls and hear the cries of the stallholders.

The apartment had a lower ceiling and was smaller and more self-contained. The old woman lived there from morning to evening, from evening to morning. And even with Honoré absent, it was clear where her place was.

He wondered for a moment if he, too, mightn't buy a dog or a cat.

It was stupid. He wasn't an old woman, or a country boy who'd come to live alone in the most populous street in Paris.

'What are you thinking about?'

He smiled.

'A dog.'

'Are you planning to buy a dog?'

'No. Anyway, it wouldn't be the same. That one was found in the street, with two paws broken.'

'Aren't you going to have a nap?'

'Unfortunately, I don't have time!'

'Anyone would say your concerns are both pleasant and unpleasant.'

He was struck by the accuracy of the observation. The death of Cuendet had made him melancholy and sorrowful. He felt a personal anger at his killers, as if Honoré had been a friend, a colleague, an old acquaintance anyway.

He was angry at them, too, for having disfigured him and thrown him, like a dead animal, on to a path in the Bois de Boulogne, where the body must have bounced on the frozen ground.

At the same time, he couldn't help smiling when thinking about Cuendet's life and obsessions, which he was making such an effort to understand. Oddly, even though they were so different from each other, he had the impression he was succeeding.

Of course, at the beginning of his career, if it could be called that, when he was merely an apprentice, Honoré had cut his teeth in the most banal way possible, the way chosen by all petty crooks born in humble circumstances, stealing whatever he could find, without discrimination.

He didn't even sell the objects he acquired in this way, but hoarded them in his garret, like a puppy hoarding crusts and old bones under its sleeping mat.

Why, when he was considered a model soldier, had he

deserted twice? Naively! Stupidly! Both times, he had let himself be caught without trying to get away or resist.

In Paris, in the Bastille neighbourhood, he had perfected his work, and his style had started to become apparent. He didn't belong to a gang. He had no friends. He worked alone.

He had been a locksmith, a boilermaker, an odd job man, and he was good with his hands, meticulous. He learned how to break into shops, workshops, warehouses.

He wasn't armed. He had never owned a weapon, not even a flick knife.

Not once had he raised an alarm, or left a trace. He was the silent man par excellence, in life as in his work.

What were his relations with women? There didn't seem to have been any in his life. He had only ever lived with his mother and, although he sometimes paid for prostitutes, he must have done so discreetly, in neighbourhoods far from home, where nobody would recognize him.

He could spend hours sitting in a café, near the window, over a bottle of white wine. He could also watch, for days on end, at the window of a furnished room, just as, in Rue Mouffetard, he would spend hours reading by the fire.

He had almost no needs. And yet the list of stolen jewels – considering only those thefts that could reasonably be attributed to him – amounted to quite a fortune.

Did he occasionally go somewhere outside Paris, where he led a different life and spent his money?

'I'm thinking', Maigret said to his wife, 'about a strange character, a burglar . . .'

'The one who was murdered this morning?'

'How did you know that?'

'It's in the midday paper that was just brought up.'

'Let me see.'

'There are only a few lines. I came across them by chance.'

A BODY IN THE BOIS DE BOULOGNE

Last night, at about three o'clock, two police officers on bicycles from the sixteenth arrondissement discovered the body of a man with a fractured skull lying on a path in the Bois de Boulogne. The man has been identified as Honoré Cuendet, born in Switzerland, fifty years old and a known criminal. According to the examining magistrate, Judge Cajou, who has been put in charge of the case and who visited the scene in the company of Deputy Prosecutor Kernavel and the pathologist, it is most likely to have been a gangland killing.

'What were you saying?'

The mention of a 'gangland killing' really upset him, because it meant that, as far as those gentlemen in the Palais de Justice were concerned, the case was practically buried. As a prosecutor had said:

'Let them kill each other, down to the last man. It's less work for the executioner and money saved for the taxpayer.'

'What was I saying? . . . Oh, yes! Imagine a burglar who deliberately chooses houses or apartments that are occupied . . .'

'To break into?'

'Yes. Every year, in Paris, every season so to speak, there are apartments that remain empty for several weeks, while their tenants are by the sea, in the mountains, in their chateaus or abroad.'

'And those apartments get burgled, is that right?'

'That's right, they get burgled. By specialists who would never dream of breaking into a place where they might find someone there.'

'What are you getting at?'

'This burglar of mine, Honoré Cuendet, is only interested in apartments that are occupied. Often, he waits until the masters have got back from the theatre or somewhere else, and the wife has taken off her jewels and put them in an adjoining room or even, sometimes, on a piece of furniture in the bedroom.'

Madame Maigret replied, logically:

'If he broke in when the wife was at a party, he wouldn't find the jewels, if, as you say, she's wearing them.'

'He'd probably find other objects of value: paintings, cash.'

'You mean that, with him, it's a kind of vice?'

'That may be too strong a word, but I suspect it was an obsession. He felt some sort of pleasure in breaking into other people's lives as they were being lived. Once, he took a stopwatch from the bedside table of a man who was sleeping. The man didn't hear a thing.'

She was smiling, too.

'How many times did you catch him?'

'He was only sentenced once, although at the time he hadn't yet adopted that technique and was stealing the same way as everyone else. But in the office we have a list of burglaries that were almost certainly his work. In some cases, he rented a room for several weeks opposite the burgled premises and had no plausible explanation for it.'

'Why was he murdered?'

'That's what I'm wondering. To know that, I need to discover what house he broke into, probably last night . . .'

He had rarely said so much to his wife about a case in progress, doubtless because, for him, it wasn't a case like any other. In fact, it wasn't even his case.

Cuendet interested him as a man and as a specialist, fascinated him almost, as did old Justine.

'I'm sure he won't leave me without anything,' she had said confidently.

And yet Maigret was convinced she didn't know where her son hid the money.

She had blind faith in her son: Honoré was incapable of leaving her penniless.

How would that money get to her? What measures had her son – a man who had never had accomplices in his life – taken to see that she was provided for?

And could he have foreseen that one day he would be murdered?

The most curious thing was that Maigret almost shared the old woman's confidence. He, too, believed that Cuendet had envisaged all possible eventualities.

He sipped at his coffee. Lighting his pipe, he glanced at the dresser. As in Rue Mouffetard, there was a carafe of spirits: in this case, sloe gin.

Madame Maigret had understood, and she poured him a little glass of it.

4.

At 3.55, bent over an annotated file beneath the circle of light from his desk lamp, Maigret was hesitating as to which pipe to fill next when the telephone rang. It was the police emergency switchboard on Boulevard du Palais.

'Hold-up in Rue La Fayette, between Rue Taitbout and Chaussée d'Antin. Gunshots exchanged. Some dead.'

It had happened at 3.50, and already a general alert had gone out, the radio cars had been alerted, and a van full of uniformed officers was leaving the courtyard of the municipal police, while, in his quiet office in the Palais de Justice, the general prosecutor, in accordance with the orders he had given, was receiving the news in his turn.

Maigret opened the door, signalled to Janvier, muttered a few more or less distinct words, and the two men descended the stairs, putting on their overcoats as they did so, and climbed into a police car.

Because of the yellowish fog that had begun to descend over the city just after lunch, it was as dark as if it were six o'clock in the evening, and the cold, instead of diminishing, had become more penetrating.

'Tomorrow morning, we'll have to look out for ice,' the driver remarked.

He put his siren on, and his flashing light. Taxis and buses were parked at the kerbs, and the pedestrians watched the police as they passed. From the Opéra onwards, the traffic was disrupted. Tailbacks had formed. Officers who had arrived as reinforcements were blowing whistles and gesticulating.

In Rue La Fayette, near the Galeries and the Printemps, this was the busiest time of day, with a dense crowd, mainly of women, on the pavements; it was also the most brightly lit place in Paris.

The crowd had been channelled, and barriers set up. One portion of the street was deserted, with only a few dark-clad officials coming and going.

The chief inspector of the tenth arrondissement had arrived with several of his men. Technicians were taking measurements and making chalk marks on the ground. There was a car with its two front wheels up on the pavement and its windscreen shattered, and two or three metres away was a dark patch, around which people were conferring in low voices.

A short, grey-haired man dressed in black, with a knitted woollen scarf around his neck, was still holding in his hand the glass of rum someone had gone to fetch him from the brasserie opposite. He was the cashier of a large household appliances store in Rue de Châteaudun.

He was telling his story for the third or fourth time, trying not to look in the direction of a human form which lay a few metres away, covered in a rough cloth.

Behind the movable barriers, like those which the city uses for processions, the crowd was pressing forward. Excited women were speaking in shrill voices.

'As I do at the end of every month . . .'

Maigret had forgotten that it was the 31st.

'. . . I'd gone to the bank behind the Opéra to collect the money to pay the staff . . .'

Maigret had seen the shop as they passed, without suspecting how big it was. The departments were spread over three floors, and there were also two basements. Three hundred people were employed there.

'I only had six hundred metres to walk. I was holding my case in my left hand.'

'Wasn't it attached to your wrist with a chain?'

He wasn't a professional collector, and no arrangements had been made for him to give the alarm, although he did have an automatic in the right-hand pocket of his overcoat.

He had crossed the street between the yellow lines and headed for Rue Taitbout, surrounded by a crowd so dense that no attack seemed possible. Suddenly, he had noticed that a man was walking very close to him, keeping pace with him. Turning his head, he had seen another man following him.

What ensued happened so fast that the cashier had barely registered it as it unfolded. What he remembered best were the words whispered in his ear:

'If you value your life, don't try to be clever!'

Simultaneously, his case was snatched violently from him. One of the men ran to a car that was coming from the opposite direction, hugging the kerb in slow motion. Hearing a shot, the cashier had at first thought that he was the one being shot at. Women screamed in panic. A second shot had been followed by the sound of broken glass.

There had been more shots, some said three, others four or five.

A red-faced man was standing to one side with the local chief inspector. He was in an emotional state, not sure yet if he was going to be called a hero or asked to account for his actions.

He was Officer Margeret, from the first arrondissement. Being off duty that afternoon, he was not in uniform. Why, then, did he have his automatic in his pocket? He would have to explain that eventually.

'I was looking for my wife, who was shopping. I witnessed the hold-up. When the three men ran to the car—'

'So there were three of them?'

'One on each side of the cashier, another behind . . .'

Officer Margeret had opened fire. One of the gang had fallen to his knees, then slowly lay down on the pavement, surrounded by the legs of the women who were starting to run.

The car had sped off in the direction of Saint-Augustin. The traffic policeman blew his whistle. There was firing from the car, which soon disappeared into the traffic.

For the next two days, Maigret would barely have time to think about his quiet Swiss. Twice when Inspector Fumel phoned him, he was too busy to answer.

They had taken the names and addresses of some fifty witnesses, including the waffle seller whose stand was nearby, an invalid who played the violin and begged in the vicinity, and two of the waiters from the café opposite, as well as the café's cashier, who claimed to have seen everything, even though the windows were steamed up.

Another man had died, a thirty-five-year-old passer-by, married with children, killed instantaneously without having any idea what was happening.

For the first time since this series of hold-ups had begun, they had a member of the gang, the one whom Officer Margeret, who by some miracle had been on the scene, had shot down.

'My idea was to shoot him in the legs, to stop him from escaping . . .'

The bullet had nevertheless hit the man in the back of the neck. He was still in a coma at the Hôpital Beaujon, where he had been taken by ambulance. Lucas, Janvier and Torrence were taking turns at the door of his room, waiting for the moment when he would finally be able to speak: the doctors hadn't given up hope of saving him.

The next day, as the driver of the police car had predicted, the streets of Paris were covered in ice. It was dark. The cars advanced very slowly. Municipal lorries were spreading sand on the main thoroughfares.

The big corridor of Quai des Orfèvres was full of people silently waiting. Maigret patiently asked each one the same questions, tracing Kabbalistic signs on a map of the area drawn up by the relevant departments.

On the evening of the hold-up, he had gone to Fontenay-les-Roses to visit the home of the gangster who had been shot down, a man named Joseph Raison, a metalworker according to his identity card.

He had found a bright, pretty apartment in a new block, a blonde young wife and two little girls of six and nine busy with their homework.

Joseph Raison, who was forty-two, really was a metal-worker and worked in a factory on Quai de Javel. He owned a 2CV and every Sunday took his family to the country.

His wife claimed to know nothing, and Maigret believed her.

'I don't see why he would have done something like that, inspector. We were happy. We bought this apartment just two years ago. Joseph was earning a good living. He didn't drink, almost never went out alone . . .'

Maigret had taken her to Beaujon, while a neighbour looked after the children. She had been able to see her husband for a few moments. Then, on the orders of the doctors and despite her insistence, she was taken back home.

Now they had to find their way through a tangle of confused and contradictory witness statements. Some had seen too much, others not enough.

'If I talk, those people will be sure to find me.'

Nevertheless, a fairly plausible description of the two men who had surrounded the cashier emerged, especially of the one who had grabbed the case.

But it was not until late in the afternoon that one of the waiters from the café thought he recognized Fernand from a photograph he was shown.

'He came into the café ten or fifteen minutes before the hold-up and ordered a café-crème. He was sitting at a table near the door, right up against the window.'

On the second day after the drama, Maigret obtained another testimony about Fernand: someone else claimed to have seen him on 31 January, dressed in a thick, brown coat.

It wasn't much, but it suggested that Maigret had not been mistaken in thinking that the ex-convict was the leader of the gang.

The injured man in Beaujon had regained consciousness for a few moments, but only to mutter:

'Monique . . .'

The name of his younger daughter.

It was another discovery that greatly interested Maigret: the fact that Fernand did not exclusively recruit his men from among the criminal classes.

The prosecutor's office was phoning him every hour, and he was sending them report after report. He couldn't leave his office without being surrounded by a swarm of reporters.

At eleven o'clock on the Friday, the corridor was at last empty. Maigret was in conversation with Lucas, who had just come back from Beaujon and was telling him about the operation that a well-known surgeon was about to attempt on the wounded man, when there was a knock at the door. He called out impatiently:

'Come in!'

It was Fumel, who, clearly feeling he had come at the wrong moment, tried to make himself very small. He must have caught a head cold, because his nose was red and his eyes watery.

'I can come back . . .'

'Come in!'

'I think I have a lead. Or rather, it's the hotel agency that found it for me. I know where Cuendet was living in the past five weeks.'

It was a relief, a relaxation almost, for Maigret to hear about his quiet Swiss.

'In which neighbourhood?'

'His old one. He had a room in a little hotel in Rue Neuve-Saint-Pierre.'

'Behind the Saint-Paul church?'

A narrow old-fashioned street between Rue Saint-Antoine and the riverside. It was rare to see a car passing there, and there were only a few shops.

'Go on.'

'Apparently, it's mainly used by prostitutes. All the same they do rent some rooms by the month. Cuendet lived there without anyone paying him much attention. He only ever went out to eat in a little restaurant called the Petit-Saint-Paul.'

'What's opposite the hotel?'

'An eighteenth-century house with a courtyard and tall windows, which was entirely restored a few years ago.'

'Who lives in it?'

'A woman on her own, with her servants, of course. Her name is Madame Wilton.'

'Did you make inquiries about her?'

'I started to, but almost nobody in the area knows anything.'

It had been the fashion for some ten years now for rich people to buy up old buildings in the Marais, in Rue des Francs-Bourgeois, for example, and restore them to something like their original state.

It had started with the Ile Saint-Louis, and now former private mansions were in demand wherever they were still available, even in the most populous streets.

'There's even a tree in the courtyard. You don't see many trees in that neighbourhood.'

'Is the woman a widow?'

'Divorced. I went to see a journalist I sometimes give tips to when there's no harm in it. This time he was the one tipping me off. Even though she's divorced, she still sees her ex-husband quite often, and they even go out together.'

'What's his name?'

'Wilton. Stuart Wilton. With his authorization, apparently, she kept his name. Her maiden name, which I found at the local police station, is Florence Lenoir. Her mother was an ironer in Rue de Rennes and her father, who's been dead a long time, was a policeman. She used to work in the theatre. According to my journalist friend, she danced with a troupe of girls at the Casino de Paris, and Stuart Wilton, who was already married, got a divorce from his first wife to marry her.'

'How long ago was that?'

Maigret was scribbling on his blotting pad, all the while imagining Honoré Cuendet at the window of the seedy little hotel.

'Only about ten years ago. The mansion belonged to Wilton. He owns another, where he lives now, in Auteuil, as well as the Château de Besse, near Maisons-Laffitte.'

'Does he own racehorses?'

'Not according to my information. He's a keen racegoer, but doesn't have a stable.'

'Is he American?'

'English. He's been living in France for a long time.'

'Where does his fortune come from?'

'I'm still just repeating to you what I've been told. He belongs to a family of big industrialists and inherited a number of patents. That brings in a lot of money without his having to do any work. He travels part of the year, rents a villa in Cap d'Antibes or Cap Ferrat every summer and belongs to a number of clubs. My journalist says he's very well known, but only within an exclusive set that doesn't often get talked about in the press.'

Maigret rose with a sigh, went and grabbed his coat from the hook and wrapped a scarf around his neck.

'Let's go!' he said.

And, to Lucas:

'If anyone asks for me, I'll be back in an hour.'

Because of the cold and the ice, the streets were almost as deserted as in August, and there wasn't a single child playing in the narrow Rue Neuve-Saint-Pierre. The half-open door of the Hôtel Lambert had a milky globe above it. In the office, which smelled musty, a man sat reading the newspaper, his back right up against the radiator.

He recognized Inspector Fumel and got to his feet, grunting:

'Hello, here comes trouble!'

'There won't be any trouble for you if you keep quiet. Is Cuendet's room occupied?'

'Not yet. He paid a month in advance. I could have let it on 31 January, but as his things are still there, I thought it best to wait.'

71

'When did he go missing?'

'I don't know. Wait while I count. Unless I'm mistaken, it must have been last Saturday . . . Saturday or Friday . . . We could ask the chambermaid.'

'Did he tell you he was going to be away?'

'He didn't say anything at all. Mind you, he never said anything.'

'The evening he went missing, did he go out late?'

'It was my wife who saw him. At night, guests who come in with a woman don't like to be let in by a man. It embarrasses them. So . . .'

'Did she tell you about it?'

'Of course she did. Anyway, you'll be able to question her later. She'll be down soon.'

The air was stagnant and overheated, and there was a dubious, all-pervasive smell, with something like a hint of disinfectant that recalled the Métro.

'From what she told me, he didn't go out to dinner that night.'

'Was that unusual?'

'It did happen sometimes. He'd buy himself something to eat. You'd see him go upstairs with little packages and newspapers. He'd say good evening, and we wouldn't hear anything more of him until the next day.'

'That evening, did he go out again?'

'He must have gone out, because he wasn't in the following morning. But, as far as seeing him goes, my wife didn't see him. She'd taken a couple up to a room at the end of the first-floor corridor. She went to look for towels, and it was then that she heard someone going down the stairs.'

'What time was that?'

'After midnight. She did intend to look and see who it was, but by the time she'd closed the linen cupboard and walked along the corridor, the man was already downstairs.'

'When did you find out he was no longer in his room?'

'The next day. Probably around ten or eleven, when the maid knocked at the door to do the cleaning. She went in and noticed that the bed hadn't been slept in.'

'Did you report the disappearance to the police?'

'Why? He was a free agent, wasn't he? He'd paid his rent. I always make them pay in advance. Sometimes people leave just like that, without saying a word.'

'Leaving their things behind?'

'He didn't exactly leave much!'

'Take us to his room.'

The owner shuffled across the floor in his slippers, left the office behind the two police officers, turned the key in the lock and put it in his pocket. He wasn't very old but he walked with difficulty and, on the stairs, they heard him breathing heavily.

'It's on the third floor,' he sighed.

There was a pile of sheets on the first-floor landing and several doors giving on to the corridor were open; somewhere, a maid was bustling about.

'It's me, Rose! I'm going up with some gentlemen.'

The smell became more sickly-sweet as they advanced. The third-floor corridor, unlike those downstairs, was uncarpeted. Someone was playing the harmonica in his room.

'It's here.'

They saw the number 33, clumsily painted on the door. The room already smelled musty.

'I've left everything as it was.'

'Why?'

'I thought he'd be back. He looked like a good man. I wonder what he was doing here, especially as he was well dressed and didn't seem to be short of money.'

'How do you know he had money?'

'Both times he paid, I saw large notes in his wallet.'

'Did he ever have any visitors?'

'Not to my knowledge, or my wife's. One of us is always in the office.'

'Not right now.'

'Of course, we do sometimes have to leave it for a few minutes, but we keep our ears open, and you noticed I told the maid.'

'Did he ever get any mail?'

'Never.'

'Who has the room next to his?'

There was only one, because number 33 was at the end of the corridor.

'Olga. A prostitute.'

The man knew that it was pointless to lie, that the police were perfectly well aware of what went on in his hotel.

'Is she in?'

'At this hour, she must be asleep.'

'You can leave us to it now.'

He walked away sullenly, dragging his feet. Maigret closed the door behind them. He began by opening a cheap wardrobe in varnished fir wood, with a lock that didn't work.

He didn't discover much: a pair of highly polished black shoes, a pair of almost new carpet slippers and a grey suit on a hanger. There was also a dark felt hat of a common brand.

In a drawer, there were shirts – six white shirts and one light blue – pants, handkerchiefs and woollen socks. In the next drawer, two pairs of pyjamas and three books: *Impressions of a Journey to Italy*, *Medicine for Everyone* (published in 1899) and an adventure novel.

The bed was of iron, the round table was covered in a dark-green velvet cloth, and the only armchair was half caved-in. The curtains, which hung from a rod, wouldn't close, but there were also net curtains that filtered the light.

Standing at the window, Maigret looked out at the house opposite, starting with the courtyard first of all, in which stood a large black car of an English make, the front steps, the double glass doors.

The stone of the façade had been cleaned up and had turned a very soft light grey. There were intricate mouldings around the windows.

A room on the ground floor was lit, revealing a carpet with a complicated pattern, a Louis XV armchair and the corner of a pedestal table.

The first-floor windows were very high, while those on the second floor were dormer windows.

When it came down to it, the mansion, which was broader than it was high, probably didn't have as many rooms as might have been thought at first sight.

Two of the first-floor windows were open, and a valet in a striped waistcoat was moving a vacuum cleaner about a room which looked like a drawing room.

'Did you get any sleep last night?'

'Yes, chief. I almost had my eight hours.'

'Are you hungry?'

'I'm not desperate yet.'

'I'll send someone to relieve you later. For now, just sit in the armchair and stay by the window. As long as you don't put the lights on, nobody can see you from the house opposite.'

Wasn't that what Cuendet had done for nearly six weeks?

'Make a note of all comings and goings, and if any cars arrive, try to get the numbers.'

A moment later, Maigret was rapping at the neighbouring door. He had to wait a while before he heard the creaking of springs, then footsteps on the floor. The door was half opened.

'What is it?'

'Police.'

'Again?'

Resigned, the woman went on:

'Come in!'

She was in her nightdress. Her eyes were swollen, and her make-up, which she hadn't taken off before going to bed, had spread, distorting her features.

'Can I go back to bed?'

'Why did you say: again? Have the police been here recently?'

'Not here, but on the streets. They've been hassling us endlessly for weeks now. I've spent at least six nights in the cells in the past month. What have I done this time?'

'Nothing, I hope. And I'd rather you didn't tell anyone about my visit.'

'Aren't you from the Vice Squad?'

'No.'

'I think I've seen your photograph somewhere.'

If it wasn't for her smudged make-up and badly dyed hair, she wouldn't have been ugly: not particularly fat, but heavy, her eyes still lively.

'Detective Chief Inspector Maigret.'

'What's going on?'

'I don't know yet. Have you lived here long?'

'Since I got back from Cannes in October. I always do Cannes in the summer.'

'Do you know your neighbour?'

'Which one?'

'The one in 33.'

'The Swiss?'

'How do you know he's Swiss?'

'Because of his accent. I worked in Switzerland two or three years ago. I was a hostess in a nightclub in Geneva, but they wouldn't renew my residence permit. I don't suppose they like the competition.'

'Did he speak to you? Did he ever come to see you?'

'I'm the one who went to him. One afternoon, I got up and realized I was out of cigarettes. I'd already passed him in the corridor, and he always said a pleasant hello to me.'

'What happened?'

She made an expressive face.

'That's just it: nothing! I knocked at the door. He took so long to open, I wondered what he was up to. But he was dressed, there was nobody with him, and the room was tidy. I saw he smoked a pipe. He had one in his mouth. I said to him:

' "I don't suppose you have any cigarettes?"

'He said no, he was sorry, then after a hesitation, he offered to go and buy me some.

'I was just like I was when I opened the door to you, with nothing on but my nightdress. There was chocolate on the table, and when he saw me looking at it, he offered me a piece.

'I thought: this was it. I mean, we're neighbours, we owe each other that. I started eating a piece of chocolate and glanced at the book he was reading, something about Italy, with old engravings.

' "Don't you get bored all on your own?" I asked him.

'I'm sure he wanted it. Not that I think I'm that impressive. There was a moment when he seemed to be on the verge, then all of a sudden he stammered:

' "I have to go out. Someone's expecting me . . ." '

'Is that all?'

'I think so. The walls aren't thick here. You can hear noises from one room to the other. And he probably didn't get much sleep at night, if you see what I mean.

'He never complained. As you may have noticed when you came up, the toilets are at the other end of the corridor, just above the stairs. There's one thing I can tell you, which is that he didn't go to bed early, because I met him at least twice, going to the toilets in the middle of the night, fully dressed.'

'Do you ever happen to look at the house opposite?'

'The madwoman's house?'

'Why do you call her the madwoman?'

'No reason. Because I think she looks mad. You know, from here, you can see everything. In the afternoon, I have nothing to do and I sometimes look out of the window. They don't usually draw the curtains in the house opposite, and it's worth a look, in the evening, to see their chandeliers. Huge crystal chandeliers, with dozens of bulbs . . .

'Her room is just opposite mine. It's just about the only room where they draw the curtains towards the end of the afternoon, but they're opened again in the morning, and then it's like she doesn't realize anyone can see her walking about stark naked. I don't know, maybe she does it deliberately. There are women who get a kick out of that.

'She has two chambermaids to take care of her, but she also rings for the valet when she's like that. Some days, the hairdresser comes in the middle of the afternoon, sometimes later, when she gets all dressed up. She isn't bad, for her age, I have to admit . . .'

'How old would you say she is?'

'About forty-five. Only, with women who look after themselves like she does, you can never be sure.'

'Does she get lots of visitors?'

'Sometimes, there are two or three cars in the court-yard, not usually more than that. Most of the time, she's the one who goes out. Apart from the gigolo, of course!'

'What gigolo?'

'I'm not saying he's a real gigolo. He's a bit young for her, not even thirty. A good-looking young man, tall, dark, dressed like a window dummy, drives a fantastic car.'

'Does he come to see her often?'

'Hey, I'm not always at the window! I have my work, too. Some days, I start at five in the afternoon. It doesn't give me much time to look at people's houses. Maybe he comes once or twice a week, maybe three times.

'What I am sure of is that he sometimes spends the night there. Usually, I get up late but, on days when I report to the police, I have to get up early in the morning. Anyone would think your colleagues deliberately choose those hours! Well, two or three times, the gigolo's car – I'll call him the gigolo – was still in the courtyard at nine o'clock.

'As for the other one . . .'

'There's another one?'

'Sure, the old one! The steady one.'

Maigret couldn't help smiling, hearing this interpretation of the facts by Olga.

'What's the matter? Did I say something stupid?'

'Carry on.'

'There's a very smart-looking guy with silvery hair who shows up sometimes in a Rolls-Royce and has the most handsome chauffeur I've ever seen.'

'Does he also sometimes spend the night there?'

'I don't think so. He never stays long. If my memory serves me well, I've never seen him late in the evening. Usually around five o'clock. Probably comes for tea . . .'

She seemed quite happy to demonstrate that she knew that some people, in a world a long way from her own, have tea at five o'clock.

'I don't suppose you can tell me why you're asking me these questions?'

'That's right, I can't.'

'And I have to keep quiet about it?'

'That's absolutely essential.'

'It's for my own good, right? Don't worry. I've heard about you from my friends, though I imagined you were older.'

She smiled at him, her body slightly arched beneath the blanket.

After a short silence, she murmured:

'No?'

And he replied with a smile:

'No.'

She burst out laughing.

'Just like my cousin!'

Then, suddenly serious:

'What has he done?'

He was on the verge of telling her the truth. He was tempted to do so. He knew he could count on her. He knew also that she was capable of understanding more things than Judge Cajou, for example. Might certain details she couldn't remember now occur to her if she was put in the picture?

Later, if it became necessary.

He headed for the door.

'Will you be back?'

'Quite likely. What's the food like at the Petit-Saint-Paul?'

'The owner's wife does the cooking. If you like *andouillettes*, you won't find any better in the neighbourhood. Only, the tablecloths are made of paper, and the waitress is a bitch.'

It was midday when he headed for the Petit-Saint-Paul. Once there, the first thing he asked for was a token so that he could phone his wife and tell her he wouldn't be back for lunch.

He hadn't forgotten about Fernand and his gang, but he couldn't help himself.

5.

It was actually a break he had given himself, as if on the sly, and he felt a touch of remorse. Not too much, though, firstly because Olga hadn't exaggerated about the *andouil-lettes*, secondly because the Beaujolais, although a little heavy, was still fruity, and finally because, sitting in a corner at a table on which a sheet of rough paper stood in for a tablecloth, he had been able to ruminate to his heart's content.

The owner's wife, who was short and fat, with a grey bun on the top of her head, occasionally half opened the kitchen door and glanced into the room. She wore an apron of the same blue as Maigret's mother had once worn, a blue that was darker at the edges and paler towards the middle where it had been rubbed more in the washing.

It was also true that the waitress, a tall brunette with a colourless complexion, was sour-faced and looked at you defiantly. From time to time, her features tensed, as if from a fleeting pain, and Maigret would have sworn that she had just had a miscarriage.

There were workers in their work clothes, a few North Africans, a woman newspaper vendor dressed in a man's jacket and cap.

What was the point of showing Cuendet's photograph to the waitress, or to the moustached owner, who was in charge of the wine? From where Maigret was sitting, which was probably where he had sat, Honoré, provided he wiped the mist from the window every three minutes, could have looked out at the street and the mansion.

He had almost certainly not confided in anyone. Like everyone else, they had taken him for a quiet little man, and in a way it was true.

Of his type, Honoré Cuendet had been a craftsman, and because Maigret was thinking at the same time about the men who had carried out the hold-up in Rue La Fayette – that was what he called ruminating – he found him a tad old-fashioned, like this restaurant in fact, which would probably soon be replaced by a brighter establishment, perhaps self-service.

Maigret had known other lone wolves, in particular the famous Commodore, who had worn a monocle and a red carnation in his buttonhole, had stayed at the most luxurious hotels, had been always impeccable and dignified beneath his white hair, and whom they had never been able to catch red-handed.

The Commodore had never set foot in prison, and nobody knew what had become of him. Had he retired to the country under a new identity, or had he seen out his final days in the sun on some Pacific island? Had he been murdered by a fellow criminal who wanted to get his hands on his accumulated wealth?

There were organized gangs at that time, too, but they didn't work in the same way. Above all, the people recruited into them were different.

Even twenty years earlier, for example, in the case of

something like the Rue La Fayette robbery, Maigret would have known immediately where to look, in which neighbourhood, even in which bistro frequented by known criminals.

In those days, they could barely read and write and wore their profession on their faces.

Now, they were technicians. The Rue La Fayette hold-up, like the previous ones, had been meticulously planned, and it had taken a chance occurrence for one of the men to be knocked out: the presence, in the crowd, of an off-duty policeman who, contrary to regulations, was armed and who, reacting instinctively, despite the risk of hitting an innocent bystander, had opened fire.

True, Honoré Cuendet had also modernized. Maigret remembered something Olga had said. She had talked about people who have tea at five o'clock. For her, it was a world apart. For Maigret, too. But Cuendet had taken the trouble to carefully study the daily routine of such people.

He didn't break windows, didn't use crowbars, didn't cause any damage.

Outside, people were walking quickly, their hands in their pockets, their faces stiff with cold, all with their own little affairs, their own little concerns in their heads, all with their personal dramas, their need to do something.

'The bill, mademoiselle.'

She scribbled the figures on the embossed paper tablecloth, moving her lips and glancing occasionally at the slate on which the prices of the dishes were written.

He walked back to the office, and as soon as he sat down at his desk, with his files and his pipes in front of him, the door opened, and Lucas came in. They both opened their mouths at the same time. Maigret spoke first.

'We need to send someone to relieve Fumel at the Hôtel Lambert in Rue Neuve-Saint-Pierre.'

Not someone belonging to what might have been called his personal team, but a man like Lourtie, for example, or Lesueur. Neither was free, and in the end it was Baron who left Quai des Orfèvres a little later with instructions.

'What about you? What were you going to say?'

'There's news. Inspector Nicolas may have got hold of something.'

'Is he here?'

'He's waiting for you.'

'Send him in.'

He was an inconspicuous man, which was why he had been sent to prowl around Fontenay-les-Roses, his mission to casually get the neighbours of the Raison family – the shopkeepers, the workers at the garage where the wounded gangster kept his car – to talk.

'I don't yet know if it means anything, chief, but I get the feeling we may have a bit of a lead. Last night, I found out that Raison and his wife were very friendly with another couple who live in the same building. In the evening, they sometimes watched television together. When they went to the cinema, one of the two women looked after the other's children along with her own.

'The name of these people is Lussac. They're younger than the Raisons. René Lussac's only thirty-one, and his wife is two or three years younger. She's very pretty, and they have a little boy of two and a half.

'So, following your instructions, I decided to keep an eye on René Lussac, who's a salesman for a musical instrument maker. He also has a car, a Floride.

'Last night, he left home after dinner, and I followed him. I had a car at my disposal. He didn't suspect I was behind him, or he'd easily have shaken me off. He went to a café at Porte de Versailles, the Café des Amis, a quiet place frequented by the local shopkeepers, who go there to play cards. Two people were waiting for him, and they played *belote* like people who see each other regularly.

'That struck me as strange. Lussac has never lived anywhere near Porte de Versailles. I wondered why he came all that way to play cards in such an unremarkable place.'

'Were you inside the café?'

'Yes. I was sure he hadn't spotted me at Fontenay-les-Roses and I wasn't taking any risks by showing my face. He didn't pay any attention to me. All three of them were playing normally, but they kept checking the time.

'At exactly nine thirty, Lussac asked the cashier for a token and went and shut himself in the phone booth, where he stayed for about ten minutes. I could see him through the window. He wasn't phoning anywhere in Paris because, after lifting the receiver once, he only said a few words and hung up. Without coming out of the booth, he waited and the phone rang a few moments later. In other words, it must have been a regional or international call.

'When he came back to the table, he seemed worried. He said a few words to them, looked around suspiciously then gestured to them to resume the game.'

'How were the two other men?'

'I went out before they did and waited in my car. I didn't think there was any point in continuing to follow Lussac, who would probably be going back to Fontenay-les-Roses. I chose one of his companions at random. Each of them had his own car. The one who looked the oldest to me was the first one to get into his car, and I followed him to a garage in Rue La Boétie. He left his car there and then walked to a building in Rue de Ponthieu, behind the Champs-Élysées, where he rents a furnished studio apartment.

'His name is Georges Macagne. I checked this morning through the hotels agency. Then I went upstairs and found his criminal record. He's been sentenced twice for car theft and once for grievous bodily harm.'

This might at last be the breakthrough they'd so long been waiting for.

'I decided not to question the owners of the café.'

'You did the right thing. I'll ask the examining magistrate for a court order, and then I want you to go to the central switchboard and ask them to find out who René Lussac phoned last night. They won't do anything without a written order.'

As Inspector Nicolas was leaving the office, Maigret called the Hôpital Beaujon, where he had a little difficulty in getting put through to the inspector on duty outside Raison's door.

'What's his condition?'

'I was just about to phone you. They went to fetch his wife. She's just arrived. I can hear her crying in his room.

Wait, the head nurse is just coming out. Will you stay on the line?'

Maigret continued to hear the muffled noises of a hospital corridor.

'Hello? It's just as I thought. He's died.'

'Did he talk?'

'He didn't even regain consciousness. His wife is lying face down on the floor in the middle of the room, crying away.'

'Did she see you?'

'Not in the state she's in.'

'Did she come by taxi?'

'I don't know.'

'Go down to the main entrance and wait. Follow her in case she tries to get in contact with someone or make a phone call.'

'Got it, chief.'

Perhaps the case was coming to an end, perhaps, thanks to that telephone call by Lussac, they were at last going to track down Fernand. It was quite logical that he would have gone to ground somewhere in the country, not far from Paris, probably one of those inns kept by retired prostitutes or former criminals.

If the telephone lead didn't yield results, they could still make the rounds of those places, although that might take a long time, and it was quite possible that Fernand, who was the brains of the gang, was changing his refuge every day.

Maigret called the examining magistrate who was dealing with the case and brought him up to date, promising him a report, which he began immediately to draw up, because the magistrate wanted to inform the prosecutor that very evening.

Among the things he put in his report was the fact that the car that had been used for the hold-up had been found near Porte d'Italie. As they had anticipated, it was a stolen car, and of course, they hadn't found anything useful in it, let alone any interesting fingerprints.

He was hard at work when the clerk, old Joseph, came and told him that the commissioner wanted to see him in his office. For a moment, he thought it might be something to do with the Cuendet case. Perhaps his chief had somehow got wind of his activities. He was fully expecting to be rapped over the knuckles.

In actual fact, it was all about a new case: the daughter of an important figure, who had been missing for three days. She was seventeen, and it had been discovered that she was secretly attending drama classes and had even been an extra in some as yet unreleased films.

'Her parents want to avoid it getting into the newspapers. There's every likelihood that she left of her own free will . . .'

He put Lapointe on the case and, as darkness fell beyond the windows, plunged back into his report.

At five o'clock, he went to see his counterpart in Special Branch, who looked like a cavalry officer. Here, there wasn't the bustle that prevailed in Maigret's department. The walls were lined with green filing cabinets, their locks as complicated as the locks of safes.

'Tell me, Danet, do you happen to know a man named Wilton?'

'Why do you ask me that?'

'Nothing very specific so far. Someone mentioned him to me, and I'd like to know a bit more about him.'

'Is he involved in a crime?'

'I don't think so.'

'You do mean Stuart Wilton?'

'Yes.'

So Danet knew him, just as he knew every foreign personality living in Paris or spending a lot of time there. Perhaps he even had a file on Wilton in those green cabinets, but he made no move to get it out.

'He's a very important man.'

'I know. Very rich, too, so I've been told.'

'Very rich, yes, and a great friend of France. In fact, he's chosen to live here for most of the year.'

'Why?'

'Firstly, because he likes the life here.'

'And what else?'

'Perhaps because he feels freer in our country than on the other side of the Channel. What intrigues me is why you're asking me these questions, because I don't see what connection there could possibly be between Stuart Wilton and your department.'

'There isn't one yet.'

'Is it because of a woman that you're interested in him?'

'It's not even true to say that I'm interested in him. There certainly is a woman who—'

'Which one?'

'He's been married several times, hasn't he?'

'Three times. And he'll probably get married again one of these days, even though he's pushing seventy.'

'So he's very fond of women?'

'Very.'

Danet was answering reluctantly, as if they were needlessly broaching questions that were his concern alone.

'I assume not only the ones he marries?'

'Naturally.'

'Is he on good terms with his last wife?'

'You mean the French one?'

'Florence, yes, the one who, so I've been told, used to be part of a dance troupe?'

'He's remained on excellent terms with her, as he has with his two previous wives. The first was the daughter of a rich English brewer, and he had a son with her. She's remarried and now lives in the Bahamas. The second was a young actress. They didn't have any children. He only lived with her for two or three years. He left her the use of a villa on the Riviera, where she lives quietly.'

'And to Florence', Maigret muttered, 'he gave a mansion.'

Danet frowned anxiously.

'Is she the one you're interested in?'

'I don't know yet.'

'She's not much in the public eye, though. Mind you, I haven't had the opportunity to study Wilton from that angle. What I know about him is what everyone says in a certain set in Paris. Florence does indeed live in one of the mansions that belonged to her former husband.'

'In Rue Neuve-Saint-Pierre.'

'That's correct. Though I'm not certain the house belongs to her. As I said, Wilton, when he divorces, remains on friendly terms with his wives, he leaves them their jewellery, their furs, but I doubt that he would leave them, as their own property, a mansion like the one you mentioned.'

'What about the son?'

'He also spends some of his time in Paris, but less than his father. He does a lot of skiing in Switzerland and Austria, takes part in motor rallies and regattas on the Riviera and in England and Italy, and plays polo.'

'In other words, he's a man of independent means.'

'Definitely.'

'Married?'

'He was, for a year, to a model, and got a divorce. Listen, Maigret, I'm not trying to outsmart you. I don't know where you're going with this, or what you have in mind. I just ask you not to do anything without telling me. When I say that Stuart Wilton is a great friend of France, it's true, and it's not for nothing that he's a Commander of the Legion of Honour. He has enormous interests here and he's a man to be treated with kid gloves.

'His private life is no concern of ours, unless he has seriously infringed the law, which would surprise me. He's a ladies' man. To be perfectly honest, I wouldn't be surprised to learn that he has some hidden vice or other. But I have no desire to know about it.

'As far as his son is concerned, and his son's divorce, I can tell you what was rumoured at the time, because you'll find out about it anyway. Lida, the model young

Wilton married, was an exceptionally beautiful girl, of Hungarian origin, unless I'm mistaken. Stuart Wilton was opposed to the marriage. The son went ahead anyway, and one fine day, he apparently realized that his wife was his father's mistress. There was no fuss. In that set, it's rare for people to make a fuss, and things are sorted out amicably. The son simply asked for a divorce.'

'And Lida?'

'What I'm telling you happened about three years ago. Since then, she's often had her photograph in the newspapers, because she's been friendly with a number of international celebrities. If I'm not mistaken, she now lives in Rome with an Italian prince. Is that what you wanted to know?'

'I have no idea.'

It was true. Maigret was tempted to put his cards on the table, to tell his colleague everything. But the two men saw things from different points of view.

With reference to what Olga had said that morning, Detective Chief Inspector Danet probably sometimes had tea at five o'clock, while Maigret, at midday today, had had lunch in a bistro with paper tablecloths, surrounded by manual workers and North Africans.

'I'll come back and speak to you again when I know a bit more. By the way, is Stuart Wilton in Paris right now?'

'Unless he's on the Riviera. I can find out. It's best if I do it.'

'And the son?'

'He lives at the Hôtel George-V, in the residential part, where he has a suite all year.'

'Many thanks, Danet.'

'Take care, Maigret.'

'I promise I will!'

He certainly wasn't going to pay a visit to Stuart Wilton and ask him questions. And if he went to the George-V, he would be answered in a polite but vague fashion.

Judge Cajou knew what he was doing in issuing his press release: the affair in the Bois de Boulogne had been a gangland slaying, which meant that there was no point in getting upset about it, or in looking too closely into it.

Some crimes cause a public stir. It depends on not very much sometimes: the personality of the victim, the way the victim was killed, even the place where it happened.

If Cuendet had been murdered in a nightclub on the Champs-Élysées, for example, he would have been entitled to a front-page headline.

But his was an almost anonymous death, without anything to retain the attention of people reading their newspapers in the Métro.

A criminal who had never committed any sensational crime and could just as easily have been fished up out of the Seine.

And yet, it was he, much more than Fernand and his gang, who interested Maigret, even though he wasn't officially allowed to get involved in the case.

When it came to the gangsters from Rue La Fayette, the whole police force had been placed on alert. But when it came to Cuendet, poor Fumet, with no car at his disposal, not even sure that he would have his taxi fare refunded if he was unfortunate enough to have to take one, was the only person investigating.

He had had to go to Rue Mouffetard, search Justine's apartment, ask questions which she had answered in her inimitable way.

All the same, once he was back in his office, Maigret phoned the Forensic Institute. Instead of asking to be put through to Dr Lamalle or one of his assistants, he preferred to speak to a laboratory worker he had known for a long time and for whom he had sometimes done favours.

'Tell me, François, did you attend the post-mortem on Honoré Cuendet, the man who was found in the Bois de Boulogne?'

'Yes, I did. Didn't you get the report?'

'I'm not in charge of the investigation, but I'd like to know.'

'I understand. Dr Lamalle thinks the victim was struck about ten times. He was first hit from behind with so much force that the skull was fractured. Death was instantaneous. You know Dr Lamalle's very good, don't you? He's not quite our old Dr Paul, of course, not yet, but everybody here already likes him.'

'What about the other blows?'

'They were to the face when the man was lying on his back.'

'What kind of instrument do they think was used?'

'They discussed it for a long time and even did a few experiments. Apparently, it wasn't a knife, and it wasn't a spanner or a tool like that, the kind that's usually used. It wasn't a crowbar either, or a club. I heard them say that whatever it was, it had a number of sharp edges. And it was heavy and solid.'

'A statuette?'

'That's the supposition they put in their report.'

'Were they able to establish the approximate time of death?'

'According to them, it was about two in the morning. Between one thirty and three, but closer to two.'

'Did he lose a lot of blood?'

'Not just blood, but brain matter as well. There was still some stuck to his hair.'

'Did they analyse the stomach contents?'

'You know what it contained? Not yet digested chocolate. There was also alcohol, though not much, which had just started entering the bloodstream.'

'Many thanks, François. If they don't ask you, don't say I phoned.'

'I'd prefer it that way, too.'

Soon afterwards, Fumel telephoned Maigret.

'I went to see the old woman, chief, and took her to the Forensic Institute. It's definitely him.'

'How did it go?'

'She was calmer than I'd feared. When I offered to take her home again, she refused and set off alone for the Métro station.'

'Did you search the apartment?'

'I didn't find anything except books and magazines.'

'No photographs?'

'A not very good photograph of the father, as a Swiss soldier, and a picture of Honoré as a baby.'

'No notes? Did you search through the books?'

'Nothing. The man didn't write letters and didn't receive any. Let alone his mother.'

'There's a lead you could follow, provided you're very careful. A man named Stuart Wilton lives in Rue de Long-champ, where he owns a mansion, I don't know the number. He has a Rolls-Royce and a chauffeur. They probably park the car in the street or keep it in a garage. Try to find out if, inside it, there's a rug made from wild-cat fur. Wilton's son lives at the George-V and also has a car.'

'Got it, chief.'

'One other thing. It'd be useful to have photographs of the two men.'

'I know a photographer who works on the Champs-Élysées.'

'Good luck!'

Maigret spent half an hour signing documents. When he left Quai des Orfèvres, instead of heading to his usual bus stop, he walked in the direction of the Saint-Paul neighbourhood.

It was still as cold and as dark, the lights of the city had a different glow from their usual one, and the silhouettes of the pedestrians were blacker, as if all shades between light and dark had been erased.

As he turned the corner of Rue Saint-Paul, a voice emerged from the darkness:

'Well, inspector?'

It was Olga, standing in a doorway, dressed in a rabbit coat. He decided to ask the girl for a piece of information he had been about to look for elsewhere, especially as she was in the best position to answer his question.

'Tell me, when you need to have a drink or warm yourself up after midnight, what's open in the neighbourhood?'

'Léon's.'

'Is it a bar?'

'Yes. In Rue Saint-Antoine, just opposite the Métro station.'

'Did you ever run into your neighbour there?'

'The Swiss? Not at night, no. Once or twice in the afternoon.'

'What was he drinking?'

'White wine.'

'Thanks.'

It was she who said to him, before pounding the pavement again:

'Good luck!'

He had a photograph of Cuendet in his pocket. He walked into the steam-filled bar and ordered a glass of cognac, and immediately regretted it on seeing six or seven stars on the bottle.

'Do you know this man?'

The owner wiped his hands on his apron before taking the photograph, which he examined with a pensive air.

'What has he done?' he asked cautiously.

'He's dead.'

'How did he die? Did he kill himself?'

'What makes you think that?'

'I don't know. I didn't see him often. Three or four times. He didn't speak to anyone. The last time . . .'

'When was that?'

'I couldn't say exactly. Last Thursday or Friday evening. Maybe Saturday. The other times, he came in the afternoon and had a drink at the counter like a man who's thirsty.'

'Just one?'

'Let's say two. No more than that. He wasn't what you'd call a drinker. I can recognize them as soon as I set eyes on them.'

'What time was it, that last evening?'

'After midnight . . . Wait . . . My wife had gone upstairs. So it must have been between half past midnight and one o'clock.'

'How come you remember so clearly?'

'First of all, at night, there's usually only the regulars, sometimes a taxi driver who's cruising . . . Or sometimes cops who come and have a drink on the sly . . . There was a couple, I remember, at the table in the corner, talking low. Apart from that, the place was empty. I was busy with my percolator. I didn't hear any footsteps. And when I turned round, he was leaning on the counter. I was quite surprised . . .'

'Is that why you remember him?'

'And also because he asked me if I had real kirsch, not kirsch-flavoured brandy. We don't serve it often. I took a bottle from the second row, this one, look, with German words on the label, and that seemed to please him. He said: "It's a good one!"'

'He took his time warming the glass in the hollow of his hand and drank slowly, looking at the time on the clock. I realized he was wondering whether to ask for another one, and when I held up the bottle, he didn't refuse. He wasn't drinking for the hell of it, but because he liked the kirsch.'

'Did he talk to anyone?'

'Only me.'

'Did the customers in the corner pay any attention to him?'

'They're lovers. I know them. They come twice a week and sit there for hours, whispering and looking each other in the eyes.'

'Did they leave soon after him?'

'Definitely not.'

'You didn't see anyone who might have been watching him from the pavement?'

The man shrugged, as if he had been insulted.

'I've been here for fifteen years . . .' he sighed.

Meaning: nothing unusual could happen without his noticing it.

Soon afterwards, Maigret walked into the Hôtel Lambert. This time, the owner's wife was in the office. She was younger and more attractive than Maigret would have predicted, having seen her husband.

'You've come about 33, haven't you? The gentleman's upstairs.'

'Thanks.'

On the stairs, he had to flatten himself against the wall to let a couple come down. The woman was wearing a lot of perfume, and the man turned his head away, embarrassed.

The room was in darkness, Baron was sitting in the

armchair he had pulled close to the window. He must have smoked a whole packet of cigarettes, because the air was stifling.

'Anything new?'

'She went out half an hour ago. Before that, a woman came to see her, carrying a large box, a linen maid or a dressmaker, I assume. They both went into the bedroom. For a while, all I could see were these two dark figures moving about, then they were still, with one of them on her knees, as if for a fitting.'

On the ground floor, the only light was in the entrance hall. The stairs were lit as far up as the second floor. On the left, two lights were still on in the drawing room, but not the big chandelier.

On the right, a chambermaid in black and white, a lace cap on her head, was tidying the boudoir.

'The kitchen and the dining room must look out on the back. Watching them, you wonder what these people do all day long. I counted at least three servants running around, obviously busy, though I couldn't see what they were busy with. Apart from the dressmaker or linen maid, there were no other visitors. The woman came in a taxi and left on foot, without her box. A delivery boy on a tricycle brought some packages. The valet took them, but didn't let him into the house. Do you want me to stay?'

'Are you hungry?'

'Just starting to get hungry, but I can wait.'

'Go.'

'Shouldn't I wait until I'm relieved?'

Maigret shrugged. What was the point?

He locked the door and slipped the key in his pocket. Downstairs, he said to the owner's wife:

'Don't let number 33 before I tell you. Nobody is to go in there, do you understand?'

In the street, he saw Olga in the distance, coming along on the arm of a man. He was pleased for her.

6.

He didn't know, as he sat down to dinner, that in a little while a telephone call would tear him away from the slightly syrupy calm of his apartment, nor that dozens of people who, at that moment, were making plans for the evening, would be spending a night different from the one they had anticipated, nor, last but not least, that until morning, all the windows at Quai des Orfèvres would remain lit up, as they were on nights of high excitement.

It was a pleasant dinner all the same, full of intimacy and a subtle understanding between his wife and himself. He had told her about the *andouillette* he had eaten for lunch in the bistro in Saint-Antoine. They had often eaten together in that type of restaurant, a type that had once been more common. Characteristic of Paris, they had been found on almost every street and were known to be frequented especially by drivers.

When it came down to it, the reason you ate well in that kind of place was that the owners all came from the provinces – the Auvergne, Brittany, Normandy, Burgundy – and had kept, not only their own local traditions, but their contacts, getting hams, cold meats, sometimes even country bread, from their own regions.

He thought of Cuendet and his mother, who had brought to Rue Mouffetard the drawling accent of the

Vaud, as well as a kind of calm, a stillness in which there was a touch of laziness.

'Any news of the old woman?'

Madame Maigret had been following his thoughts in his eyes.

'You're forgetting that officially my main concern at the moment is these hold-ups. They're more serious, because they're a threat to banks, insurance companies and big businesses. The gangsters have modernized faster than we have.'

It was a passing fit of depression. Or more precisely, of nostalgia; his wife knew that, and she knew, too, that it never lasted very long.

At such moments, anyway, he was less afraid of retirement, which was just two years away. The world was changing, Paris was changing, everything was changing, men and methods. Retirement might seem frightening, but if he didn't retire, wouldn't he end up adrift in a world he no longer understood?

Nevertheless, he ate heartily and slowly.

'She's a strange character! There'd been nothing to suggest what happened to him, and yet when I expressed concern for her future, his mother just said: "I'm sure he won't leave me without anything."'

If that was true, how had Cuendet arranged things, what kind of scheme had he worked out in that big ruddy head of his?

It was at that moment, as Maigret was beginning his dessert, that the telephone rang.

'Shall I answer it?'

He was already standing, his napkin in his hand. He was being called from the office. It was Janvier.

'This may be important, chief. Inspector Nicolas has just called. They've been able to trace the call made by René Lussac from the café at Porte de Versailles. It's a number in the Corbeil area, a villa on the banks of the Seine, which belongs to someone you know, Rosalie Bourdon.'

'The lovely Rosalie?'

'Yes. I called the Flying Squad at Corbeil. The woman's at home.'

Someone else who had spent many hours in Maigret's office. She was pushing fifty now, but was still an attractive woman, well built, with a florid complexion and an obscenely picturesque way of expressing herself.

She had started very young, walking the streets around Place des Ternes. By the age of twenty-five, she was running a brothel frequented by the most distinguished men in Paris.

Later, in Rue Notre-Dame-de-Lorette, she had run a nightclub of a specialized kind called Le Cravache – The Whip.

Her last lover, the love of her life, was a man named Pierre Sabatini, from the Corsican gang, sentenced to twenty years' hard labour for killing two members of the Marseille gang in a bar in Rue de Douai.

Sabatini was still in Saint-Martin-de-Ré, and had several years of his sentence to go. Rosalie's attitude at the trial had moved everyone, and when sentence had been pronounced, she had moved heaven and earth to obtain authorization to marry her lover.

It had been in all the newspapers. She had claimed she was pregnant. Some had assumed that she had got herself pregnant by the first man who came along just in order to secure this marriage.

In fact, when the ministry had refused, her pregnancy was forgotten about. Rosalie had disappeared from the scene, withdrawing to her villa near Corbeil, from where she regularly sent Sabatini letters and parcels. Every month she travelled to Ile de Ré to visit him, and she was closely watched, for fear she was planning her lover's escape.

As it happened, Sabatini had shared a cell in Saint-Martin with Fernand.

Janvier continued:

'I asked Corbeil to keep an eye on the villa. It's being surrounded right now.'

'What about Nicolas?'

'He asked me to tell you he's on his way to Porte de Versailles. Judging by what he saw yesterday, his impression is that Lussac and his two friends meet there every evening. He wants to get to the café before they do. That way he's less likely to attract their attention.'

'Is Lucas still in the office?'

'He's just come in.'

'Tell him to keep a certain number of men available tonight. I'll call you back in a few minutes.'

He phoned the prosecutor's office but was only put through to the deputy on duty.

'I'd like to speak to Prosecutor Dupont d'Hastier.'

'He isn't here.'

'I know. But I need to speak to him urgently. It's about the latest hold-ups, probably about Fernand, too.'

'I'll try and get in touch with him. Are you at the office?'

'No, I'm at home.'

He gave his number and, from that point on, things moved rapidly. He had barely finished his dessert when the telephone rang again. It was the prosecutor.

'I hear you've arrested Fernand?'

'Not yet, sir, but we may have a chance to arrest him tonight.'

In a few sentences, he brought him up to date.

'Can you meet me in my office in a quarter of an hour? I'm dining with friends, but I'm leaving right now. Have you been in touch with Corbeil?'

Madame Maigret was making him some very black coffee and taking out the bottle of raspberry liqueur from the sideboard.

'Make sure you don't catch cold. Do you think you'll be going to Corbeil?'

'I'd be surprised if they gave me the chance.'

He wasn't mistaken. At the Palais de Justice, in one of the vast offices of the prosecutor's office, he found, not only Prosecutor Dupont d'Hastier, in a dinner jacket, but Judge Legaille, the examining magistrate in charge of the case, as well as one of his old friends from the other place, the Sûreté, Detective Chief Inspector Buffet.

Buffet was taller, broader and heavier than Maigret, with a ruddy complexion and eyes that always looked sleepy, and yet he was one of the most formidable police officers around.

'Sit down, Maigret, and tell us how things stand.'

Before leaving Boulevard Richard-Lenoir, he had had another telephone conversation with Janvier.

'I'm waiting for news any moment. But what I can tell you is that there's been a man in Rosalie Bourdon's villa in Corbeil for some days now.'

'Have our officers seen him?' asked Buffet, who had a very small voice for such a large body, almost a girl's voice.

'Not yet. They've talked to some of the neighbours, and the description they give matches Fernand's.'

'Have they surrounded the villa?'

'At a distance, in order not to raise the alarm.'

'Are there several ways out?'

'Of course. But there are other developments. As I told the prosecutor on the phone earlier, Lussac is a friend of Joseph Raison, the gangster who was killed in Rue La Fayette, and was living in the same building as him in Fontenay-les-Roses. Lussac and at least two friends frequent a café at Porte de Versailles, the Café des Amis. They were playing cards last night, and at nine thirty Lussac went to the phone booth and called Corbeil.

'That seems to be the way the three men stay in touch with their boss. I'm waiting for a phone call any moment now. If they meet at the same place this evening, which we'll soon know, then we have a decision to make.'

In the old days, he would have made it himself, and this war council in the offices of the prosecutor's office would not have taken place. It would even have been unthinkable, unless they were dealing with something political.

'According to a witness, when the hold-up happened,

Fernand was in a brasserie just opposite the spot where the cashier was assaulted and where his assailants, minus one, jumped in a car with a case containing millions of francs. Given the unexpected thing that happened, it's unlikely that Fernand has been able to meet up with them. If he's the one who's hiding out with the lovely Rosalie, he must have gone to ground there that same evening, and every evening since then he's been in touch with the Café des Amis to give his instructions.'

Buffet was listening, although he seemed asleep. Maigret knew that his colleague from the Sûreté thought the same way he did, envisaged the same possibilities, the same dangers. It was not for the sake of the gentlemen in the prosecutor's office that he was supplying so many details.

'Sooner or later, one of the men will be given the task of taking all or part of the loot to Fernand. Obviously, if that happens, we'll have conclusive proof. But we may have to wait several days, and in the meantime, it's possible that Fernand might look for another retreat. Even with the villa surrounded, he's quite capable of slipping through our fingers.

'On the other hand, if the three men meet at the Café des Amis this evening, as they did yesterday, we have the possibility of arresting them simultaneously with getting our hands on Fernand in Corbeil.'

The telephone rang. The clerk of the court passed the receiver to Maigret.

'It's for you.'

It was Janvier, who had become a kind of go-between.

'They're there, chief. What have you decided?'

'I'll let you know in a few minutes. Send one of our men to Fontenay-les-Roses with a social worker. Ask him to phone you once he's there.'

'Got it.'

Maigret hung up.

'What have you decided, gentlemen?'

'Not to take any risks,' the prosecutor said. 'We'll get evidence in the end, won't we?'

'They'll hire the best lawyers, they'll refuse to talk, and they've probably already fabricated excellent alibis.'

'On the other hand, if we don't arrest them this evening, we may never have a chance to arrest them again.'

'I'll take care of Corbeil,' Buffet announced.

Maigret couldn't object to that. It was outside his jurisdiction and was a matter for the Sûreté.

'Do you think they'll open fire?' the examining magistrate asked.

'If they have the opportunity, it's pretty much certain they will, but we'll try not to give them the chance.'

A few minutes later, Maigret and Buffet passed from one world to another, simply by walking through the door separating the Palais de Justice from the headquarters of the Police Judiciaire.

Here, the excitement of one of their important days was already tangible.

'Before we move in on the villa, I think we should wait to see if there's a phone call at nine thirty.'

'I agree. But I'd prefer to be there in advance, in order to get everything ready. I'll call you to find out how things stand.'

In the dark, cold courtyard, there was already a radio car with its engine being warmed up and a van full of police officers. The chief inspector for the sixteenth arrondissement was somewhere near the Café des Amis, with all his available men.

In the café, shopkeepers were calmly talking about their business and playing cards, not suspecting a thing. Nobody noticed Inspector Nicolas, who was sitting reading his newspaper.

He had just phoned and said laconically:

'We're on.'

That meant that the three men were there, as they had been the day before, René Lussac sometimes glancing at his watch, presumably in order not to miss his nine-thirty call to Corbeil.

There, men waited in the darkness, surrounded by patches of ice, watching the villa, where two windows on the ground floor were lighted.

The central switchboard was also on the alert. At 9.35, the announcement came:

'He's just asked for Corbeil.'

And an inspector on the wire-tap recorded the conversation.

'How are things?' Lussac asked.

It wasn't a man who replied, but Rosalie.

'Fine, nothing new.'

'Jules is impatient.'

'Why?'

'He wants to go travelling.'

'Stay on the line.'

She must have been conferring with someone. Then she came back to the phone.

'He says we have to keep waiting.'

'Why?'

'Because we have to!'

'People are starting to get suspicious here.'

'Hold on.'

Another silence, then:

'There'll be news tomorrow.'

Buffet called from Corbeil.

'Well?'

'It's done. Lussac made his call. It was the woman who replied, but there was someone next to her. Apparently, a man named Jules, who's a member of the gang, is starting to get impatient.'

'Shall we go?'

'At ten fifteen.'

The two actions had to be simultaneous in order to avoid the possibility that one of the men might miraculously escape the net on Avenue de Versailles and warn Corbeil.

'Ten fifteen.'

Maigret gave his last instructions to Janvier.

'When Fontenay-les-Roses calls, have Madame Lussac arrested, whether or not there's a warrant. Have her brought here, and leave the social worker to take care of the child.'

'What about Madame Raison?'

'Not her. Not yet.'

Maigret took his place in the radio car. The van had

already left. At Porte de Versailles, a few passers-by were startled by the unusual activity in the area, men hugging the houses and talking in low voices, others vanishing into dark corners as if by magic.

Maigret contacted the chief inspector from the sixteenth arrondissement, and the two of them finalized the details of the operation.

Once again there were two courses of action to choose from. They could wait for the three card players, who could be seen through the windows of the café, to come out and head for their respective cars.

That seemed like the simpler solution. And yet it was the more dangerous of the two, because once they were outside, the men would have freedom of movement and perhaps time to open fire. In the heat of a shoot-out, wasn't there the possibility that one of them might jump in his car and get away?

'Is there another exit?'

'There's a door leading out to the yard, but the walls are high and the only way out is through the corridor of the building.'

It took no more than a quarter of an hour for the men to get into position, and the attention of the customers in the Café des Amis was not aroused.

Men who could pass for tenants entered the building. Some of them took up positions in the yard.

Three others, pretending to be drunken merrymakers, opened the door of the café and sat down at the table next to the card players.

Maigret looked at his watch, like a general waiting for

zero hour. At 10.40, he opened the door to the café, alone. He had his knitted scarf around his neck and his right hand in the pocket of his overcoat.

He only had two metres to walk. The gangsters didn't even have time to stand up. Standing close to them, he said in a low voice:

'Don't move. You're surrounded. Keep your hands on the table.'

Inspector Nicolas had approached.

'Handcuff them. You others, too.'

With an abrupt movement, one of the men managed to knock over the table. There was a noise of broken glass, but two inspectors already had him by the wrists.

'Outside.'

Maigret turned to the customers.

'Don't worry, ladies and gentlemen. A simple police operation.'

Fifteen minutes later, the three men were taken out of the van and each was led into an office at Quai des Orfèvres.

Corbeil was on the line, Buffet's thin voice.

'Maigret? It's done.'

'No hitches?'

'He did manage to open fire. One of my men was hit in the shoulder.'

'What about the woman?'

'My face is covered in scratches. I'll bring them in as soon as I've finished with the formalities.'

The telephone wouldn't stop ringing. This time, it was the prosecutor.

'Yes, sir. We have them all . . . No, I haven't asked them a single question yet. I put them in separate offices, and I'm waiting for the man and woman Buffet is bringing me from Corbeil.'

'Be careful. Don't forget that they'll claim the police manhandled them.'

'I know.'

'Or that they have an absolute right to say nothing without the presence of a lawyer.'

'Yes, sir.'

Maigret didn't have any intention of questioning them immediately anyway, preferring to let them stew in their own juice. He was waiting for Madame Lussac.

She did not arrive until eleven, because she had been in bed when the inspector arrived and it had taken her time to get dressed and explain to the social worker what needed to be done for her son.

She was a short, thin, quite pretty brunette, barely more than twenty-five. She was pale, with pinched nostrils. She said nothing, avoiding playing the part of the indignant wife.

Maigret sat her down in front of him, while Janvier installed himself at the end of the desk with pencil and paper.

'Your husband's name is René Lussac, and he's a sales representative?'

'Yes, monsieur.'

'He's thirty-one years old. How long have you been married?'

'Four years.'

'What's your maiden name?'

'Jacqueline Beaudet.'

'Born in Paris?'

'No, in Orléans. I came to Paris when I was sixteen to live with my aunt.'

'What does your aunt do?'

'She's a midwife. She lives in Rue Notre-Dame-de-Lorette.'

'Where did you meet René Lussac?'

'In a shop selling records and musical instruments where I worked as an assistant. Where is he, inspector? Tell me what's happened to him. Ever since Joseph—'

'Do you mean Joseph Raison?'

'Yes. Joseph and his wife were our friends. We live in the same building.'

'Did the two men go out a lot together?'

'Sometimes. Not often. Ever since Joseph died . . .'

'You're afraid the same thing might happen to your husband, aren't you?'

'Where is he? Has he disappeared?'

'No. He's here.'

'Alive?'

'Yes.'

'Hurt?'

'He almost was, but he isn't.'

'Can I see him?'

'Not right away.'

'Why not?' She gave a bitter smile. 'Stupid of me to ask you that question! I can guess what you're looking for, why you're questioning me. You're telling yourself it'll be easier to make a woman talk than a man, aren't you?'

'Fernand has been arrested.'

'Who's Fernand?'

'Do you really not know?'

She looked him in the eyes.

'No. My husband's never mentioned him. All I know is that someone gives the orders.'

Although she had taken a handkerchief from her bag, because she thought it was the thing to do, she wasn't crying.

'You see, it's easier than you imagined. I've been afraid for quite a long time now, and I've been begging René not to see these people any more. He has a good job. We were happy. Although we weren't rich, we didn't have a bad life. I don't know who it was he met . . .'

'How long ago?'

'About six months. It was towards the end of summer . . . I wish it were all over, because then I wouldn't have to be scared any more. Are you sure that woman will be able to take care of my son?'

'You have nothing to fear in that respect.'

'He's a nervous boy, like his father. He gets restless at night . . .'

It was obvious she was exhausted and rather lost, and was making an effort to get her thoughts in order.

'What I can tell you is that René didn't shoot.'

'How do you know that?'

'First of all, because he'd be incapable of it. He let those people lead him on. He never imagined it would get so serious.'

'Did he talk to you about it?'

'For a while I'd seen that he was bringing back more money than he should have. He also went out more, almost always with Joseph Raison. One day, I found his automatic.'

'What did he say?'

'That I shouldn't worry, that in a few months we'd be able to go and live quietly in the South. He wanted to start his own business, in Cannes or Nice . . .'

At last she was crying, noiselessly, with little sobs.

'Basically, it was all because of the car. He absolutely had to have a Floride. He made a down payment. Then the time came to start paying the instalments . . . When he finds out I've talked, he'll be angry with me. Maybe he won't want to live with me any more.'

There was noise in the corridor, and Maigret motioned to Janvier to take the young woman into the next office. He had recognized Buffet's voice.

Three men pushed a fourth man into the room, a man with handcuffs on his wrists, who immediately gave Maigret a defiant look.

'Where's the woman?' Maigret asked.

'At the other end of the corridor. She's more dangerous than he is, she scratches and bites.'

Buffet had a scratched face and blood on his neck to prove it.

'Come in, Fernand.'

Buffet came in, too, while the two inspectors remained outside. Fernand looked around him at the room and said:

'I think I've been here before.'

He was regaining his self-confidence and his sardonic demeanour.

'I suppose you're going to wear me down with questions, like the last time. I can tell you right now that I won't answer.'

'Who's your lawyer?'

'Same one as before. Maître Gambier.'

'Do you want us to call him?'

'Personally, I have nothing to say to him. If you find it amusing to drag the man out of his bed . . .'

All night at Quai des Orfèvres, there were comings and goings in the corridors and from office to office. There was the rattle of typewriters. The telephone rang constantly, because the prosecutor's office was determined to keep in touch, and the examining magistrate hadn't gone to bed.

One of the inspectors spent most of his time making coffee. From time to time, Maigret would meet one of his colleagues between offices.

'Still nothing?'

'He's keeping quiet.'

None of the three men from the Café des Amis admitted to recognizing Fernand. They were all playing the same game.

'Who's he?'

And when they were played a recording of the call to Corbeil, they would reply:

'That's René's business. His love affairs are no concern of ours.'

René himself replied:

'I'm entitled to have a mistress, aren't I?'

They brought Madame Lussac in to confront Fernand.

'Do you recognize him?'

'No.'

'What did I tell you?' Fernand said triumphantly. 'These people have never seen me. I came out of Saint-Martin-de-Ré without a cent, and a friend gave me the address of his girlfriend, telling me she'd give me something to eat. I was staying in her house, simple as that.'

Maître Gambier arrived at one in the morning and immediately raised points of law.

According to the new code of criminal procedure, the police couldn't detain these men for more than twenty-four hours, after which the case would be taken over by the prosecutor's office and the examining magistrate, who would decide whether or not to proceed.

They could already sense doubts growing in the Palais de Justice.

The confrontation between Madame Lussac and her husband yielded nothing.

'Tell them the truth.'

'What truth? That I have a mistress?'

'The automatic . . .'

'A pal gave me an automatic. So what? I'm often on the road, travelling alone at the wheel of my car . . .'

Once morning came, they would start searching for witnesses, all those who had already been through Quai des Orfèvres: the café waiters from Rue La Fayette, the cashier, the beggar, the off-duty police officer who had opened fire.

Also once morning came, they would search the apartments of the three men arrested at Porte de Versailles. Perhaps they would find the case with the money in one of them.

It was all a matter of routine, a somewhat sickening, taxing routine.

'You can go back to Fontenay-les-Roses, but the social worker will stay with you until further orders.'

He had her driven back there. She was ready to drop, and she looked around her with startled eyes, as if she no longer knew where she was.

While his men continued to bombard the prisoners with questions, Maigret went out for a walk. The first snowflakes fell on his hat and his shoulders. A bar was just opening its doors on Boulevard du Palais, and he stood at the counter, ate some warm croissants and drank two or three cups of coffee.

When he got back to the office at seven, sluggish and blinking in the light, he was surprised to find Fumel there.

'What do you have for me now?'

Fumel, who was very excited, began talking volubly.

'I was on duty last night. I was kept up to date with what you were doing on Avenue de Versailles, but as I wasn't involved I took the opportunity to phone a few friends from the other arrondissements. They've all had the photograph of Cuendet by now. I told myself that one of these days something might come of it . . .

'Anyway, I was chatting to Duffieux from the eighteenth and I mentioned Cuendet. And Duffieux told me he'd been just about to phone me on that very subject. He works with a friend of yours, Inspector Lognon. When Lognon saw the photograph yesterday morning, he immediately made a face and stuffed it in his pocket without saying a word. Cuendet's face looked familiar to him. Apparently, he started asking questions in the bars and little restaurants in Rue Caulaincourt and Place Constantin-Pecqueur.

'You know when Lognon gets an idea in his head, he can't let go of it. He ended up knocking at the right door, just at the top of Rue Caulaincourt, a brasserie called the Régence. They recognized Cuendet without hesitation and told Lognon he came there quite often with a woman.'

'How long had that been going on?' Maigret asked.

'Well, that's the most interesting part. For years, according to them.'

'Do they know the woman?'

'The waiter doesn't know her name, but he's sure she lives locally, because he sees her pass by every morning on her way to do her shopping.'

The whole of the Police Judiciaire was busy with Fernand and his gang. In two hours, the corridors would again be overflowing with witnesses to whom the four men would be presented in turn. It would take all day, and the typewriters would be constantly spewing out the transcripts of statements.

In the middle of this agitation that had nothing to do with him, only Inspector Fumel, his fingers stained with nicotine from the cigarettes he smoked to the very end, to the point that they had left an indelible mark above his lip, only Fumel was talking to Maigret about the quiet Swiss whom everyone else had forgotten.

Wasn't that case dead and buried? Wasn't Judge Cajou convinced he wouldn't have to deal with it any more?

He had uttered his verdict on the first day:

'A gangland killing.'

He didn't know old Justine, or the apartment in Rue Mouffetard, let alone the Hôtel Lambert and the sumptuous mansion opposite.

'Are you tired?'

'Not too much.'

'Shall we both go?'

Maigret's tone was almost conspiratorial, as if he had suggested they both play truant.

'By the time we get there, it'll be day.'

He left instructions for his men, stopped at the corner to buy tobacco and, accompanied by Fumel, who was shivering with cold, waited for the bus to Montmartre.

7.

Did Lognon suspect that Maigret attached more importance to the almost anonymous corpse in the Bois de Boulogne than to the hold-up in Rue La Fayette and the gang who would be all over the newspapers the next day?

If he did, would he have followed the thread he had picked up? And in that case, God alone knew how far he would have gone to discover the truth, because he was probably the police officer with the most highly developed sixth sense in Paris, the most stubborn, too, and the one who most desperately wanted to succeed.

Was it bad luck that stood in his way, or the belief that fate had it in for him, that when it came down to it he was destined always to be a victim?

The fact remained, he would end his career as an inspector in the eighteenth arrondissement, just as Aristide Fumel would in the sixteenth. Fumel's wife had left without leaving a forwarding address; Lognon's was ill, and had spent the last fifteen years complaining.

As far as the Cuendet case was concerned, it had all happened rather stupidly. Lognon, busy with something else, had passed the tip on to a colleague, who in turn had only attached enough importance to it to mention it in passing during his telephone conversation with Fumel.

The snow was falling quite heavily now and was

starting to settle on the roofs, although unfortunately not on the streets. Maigret was always disappointed to see the snow melt on the pavement.

The bus was overheated. Most of the travellers were quiet and looked straight ahead, their heads swaying from side to side, fixed expressions on their faces.

'Anything new on the rug?'

Fumel, who had been lost in thought, gave a start and echoed as if he didn't immediately understand:

'The rug?'

He, too, hadn't slept enough.

'The wildcat fur rug.'

'I looked in Stuart Wilton's car. I didn't see any rug. Not only does the car have heating, it has air conditioning. It even has a little bar, a garage mechanic told me that.'

'What about his son's car?'

'He generally parks it outside the George-V. I took a glance at it. I didn't see any rug there either.'

'Do you know where he gets his petrol?'

'Usually at a garage in Rue Marbeuf.'

'Did you go there?'

'I didn't have time.'

The bus stopped at the corner of Place Constantin-Pecqueur. The pavements were practically empty. It wasn't yet eight in the morning.

'That must be the brasserie.'

The lights were on, and a waiter was sweeping sawdust off the floor. It was an old-fashioned brasserie, of the kind that were less and less common in Paris, with round metal holders for the napkins, a marble counter where a cashier probably sat behind the till, and mirrors all around the walls. There were signs up, recommending the *choucroute garnie* and the *cassoulet*.

The two men went inside.

'Have you eaten?'

'Not yet.'

Fumel ordered coffee and brioches, while Maigret, who had already drunk too much coffee during the night and whose tongue felt coated, ordered a little glass of brandy.

Outside, it was as if life were finding it difficult to get into gear. It was neither night nor day. Children on their way to school were trying to grab snowflakes that must have tasted like dust.

'Tell me, waiter . . .'

'Yes, monsieur?'

'Do you know this man?'

The waiter looked at Maigret with a knowing air.

'You're Monsieur Maigret, aren't you? I recognize you. You came here two years ago with Inspector Lognon.'

He examined the photographs smugly.

'He's a customer, yes. He always comes with the little lady with the hats.'

'Why do you call her the little lady with the hats?'

'Because she always wears different hats, these funny little fascinators. Mostly they come in to have dinner. They sit in the corner over there, right at the far end. They're nice. She loves the *choucroute*. They take their time, have coffee after the meal, then have a little drink and hold hands.'

'Have they been coming here long?'

'Years. I don't know how many.'

'Apparently, she lives locally?'

'I've already been asked that question. She must have an apartment in one of the buildings nearby, because I see her pass almost every morning with her shopping bag.'

Why was Maigret delighted to discover a woman in Honoré Cuendet's life?

Soon afterwards, he and Fumel walked into the concierge's lodge of the first building. The mail was just being sorted.

'Do you know this man?'

She looked closely at the photograph and shook her head.

'I think I've seen him before, but I can't say I know him. Anyway, he's never been here.'

'You don't have, among your tenants, a woman who often changes her hats?'

She looked at Maigret in astonishment, shrugged her shoulders and muttered something he didn't understand.

They were no more successful in the second building, or in the third. In the fourth, the concierge was bandaging her husband's hand after he had cut it taking out the dustbins.

'Do you know this man?'

'What of it?'

'Does he live here?'

'Not exactly. He's a friend of the little lady on the fifth floor.'

'What little lady?'

'Madame Evelyne, the milliner.'

'Has she lived here long?'

'At least twelve years. She was already here when I started.'

'Was he already her friend then?'

'He might have been. I don't remember.'

'Have you seen them lately?'

'Who? Her? I see her every day!'

'What about him?'

'Do you remember the last time he came, Désiré?'

'No, but it was quite a while ago.'

'Did he sometimes spend the night?'

She seemed to find Maigret naive.

'What of it? They're adults, aren't they?'

'Did he stay here for several days on end?'

'Even weeks sometimes.'

'Is Madame Evelyne in? What's her surname?'

'Schneider.'

'Does she get a lot of post?'

The bundle of letters in front of the pigeon-holes hadn't yet been untied.

'Almost none.'

'Fifth floor on the left?'

'On the right.'

Maigret went out into the street to see if there was any light at the windows and, as there was, he set off up the stairs with Fumel. There was no lift. The staircase was well maintained, the house clean and quiet, with mats in front of the doors and the odd brass or enamel name plate.

They noted a dentist on the second floor, a midwife on

the third. Maigret stopped from time to time to catch his breath. He heard a radio playing somewhere.

On the fifth floor, he almost hesitated before ringing the bell. There was a radio playing in this apartment, too, but it was switched off and footsteps approached the door, which opened. Quite a short woman, with light-blonde hair and blue eyes, dressed not in a dressing gown but a kind of smock, peered out at them, a cloth in her hand.

Maigret and Fumel were as embarrassed as she was, because they could see first the surprise, then the fear grow in her eyes. Her lips quivered, and at last she said in a low voice:

'Have you come to give me bad news?'

She motioned them into the living room she had been cleaning and pushed away the vacuum cleaner that was in their way.

'Why do you ask that?'

'I don't know . . . A visit, at this hour, when Honoré has been away for so long . . .'

She was about forty-five but looked a lot younger. Her skin was smooth, her figure rounded and firm.

'Are you police?'

'Detective Chief Inspector Maigret. This is Inspector Fumel.'

'Has Honoré had an accident?'

'You're right, I have bad news for you.'

She wasn't crying yet and they could sense her trying to cling to trivia.

'Sit down. Take off your coats, it's very hot in here. Honoré likes it hot. Sorry it's so untidy . . .'

'Do you love him a lot?'

She was biting her lips, trying to guess how serious the news was.

'Is he hurt?'

Then almost immediately:

'Is he dead?'

She wept at last, her mouth open like a child's, with no fear of looking ugly. At the same time, she grasped her hair in both hands and looked around her as if searching for a corner in which to take shelter.

'I always had a feeling something like this would happen.'

'Why?'

'I don't know . . . We were too happy . . .'

The room was comfortable and intimate, with solid furniture of good quality and a few trinkets which weren't in excessively bad taste. Through an open door, they could see a bright kitchen, where the table had been laid for breakfast.

'Take no notice of me . . .' she kept saying. 'I'm sorry . . .'

She opened another door. It led to the unlit bedroom, where she threw herself across the bed, flat on her stomach, to cry freely.

Maigret and Fumel looked at each other in silence. Of the two, Fumel was the more moved, perhaps because he had never been able to resist women, in spite of the trouble they had caused him.

It didn't last as long as they might have feared. She went into the bathroom and ran some water, and when she came back, her face was almost relaxed.

'I do apologize,' she said. 'How did it happen?'

'He was found dead in the Bois de Boulogne. Haven't you read the papers in the last few days?'

'I don't read the papers. But why the Bois de Boulogne? What was he doing there?'

'He was murdered somewhere else.'

'Murdered? For what reason?'

She made an effort not to burst into tears again.

'Had you been friends for a long time?'

'More than ten years.'

'Where did you meet?'

'In a brasserie near here.'

'The Régence?'

'Yes. It was a place I occasionally ate in. I noticed him sitting alone in his corner.'

Didn't that suggest that Cuendet had been preparing a burglary in the neighbourhood around that time? Probably. Examining the lists of unsolved robberies, they might well find one committed in Rue Caulaincourt.

'I don't remember how we got talking. But anyway, one evening, we had dinner at the same table. He asked me if I was German, and I told him I was from Alsace. I was born in Strasbourg.'

She gave a wan smile.

'We both laughed at each other's accents. He'd kept his Swiss accent the way I've kept mine.'

It was a pleasant, singsong accent. Madame Maigret was also from Alsace and was more or less the same height, with the same slightly stout figure.

'And you became friends?'

She wiped her nose without concern for how red it was getting.

'He wasn't always here. He seldom spent more than two or three weeks with me, then he'd go travelling. I wondered at first if he didn't have a wife and children in the provinces. Some provincials take off their wedding rings when they come to Paris.'

She gave the impression she had known other men before Cuendet.

'How did you know that wasn't the case with him?'

'He wasn't married, was he?'

'No.'

'I was sure of it. First of all, I realized he didn't have any children of his own from the way he looked at other children in the street. You could see he was resigned not to be a father, but there was a kind of longing there. And when he stayed here, he didn't behave like a married man. It's hard to explain. He had a modesty about him that married men tend to lose. The first time we slept together, for example, I realized he was embarrassed to find himself in my bed, and he was even more embarrassed when he woke up the next morning . . .'

'Did he ever tell you about his profession?'

'No.'

'Did you ever ask him about it?'

'I did try to find out, though I didn't want to be indiscreet.'

'He told you that he travelled?'

'That he needed to go away. He never told me where he was going, or why. One day, I asked him if his mother was still alive, and he blushed. That made me think that he was living with her. In any case, he had someone to mend his underwear and darn his socks, someone who didn't do it very well. His buttons were always badly sewn on, for example, and I used to tease him about it.'

'When did he leave you for the last time?'

'Six weeks ago. I could find the date . . .'

Now she asked:

'When did . . . when did it happen?'

'On Friday.'

'But he never had much money on him.'

'When he came to spend time with you, did he bring a suitcase?'

'No. If you look in the wardrobe, you'll find his dressing gown and his slippers there, and his shirts, socks and pyjamas in a drawer.'

She pointed at the mantelpiece, and Maigret saw three pipes, including one meerschaum. Here, too, there was a coal stove, as in Rue Mouffetard, and an armchair beside it, Honoré Cuendet's armchair.

'Please forgive my indiscretion, but there's a question I'm obliged to ask you.'

'I can guess what it is. You want to ask me about money.'

'Yes. Did he give you any?'

'He offered to give me money. I didn't accept it, because I make a good living. All I allowed him to do, because he insisted and because he felt uncomfortable living here without paying his share, was to pay half the rent. He did give me gifts. He was the one who bought the furniture in this room and set up my fitting room. You can see it . . .'

A narrow room, with Louis XVI furniture and a profusion of mirrors.

'He's also the one who repainted the walls, including those in the kitchen, and papered the living room, because he loved doing odd jobs.'

'How did he spend his days?'

'He walked a bit, not very much, and always the same route, just around the neighbourhood, like someone walking his dog. Apart from that, he'd sit in his armchair and read. You'll find heaps of books in the wardrobe, almost all travel books.'

'Did you ever travel with him?'

'We spent a few days in Dieppe, the second year. Another time, we went on holiday to Savoy, and he showed me the Swiss mountains in the distance, saying that was his country. Another time again, we went from Paris to Nice by coach and visited the Riviera.'

'Was he a big spender?'

'That depends what you call big. He wasn't stingy, but he didn't like it when people tried to cheat him and he'd often send back hotel and restaurant bills.'

'Are you over forty?'

'I'm forty-four.'

'So you have a certain amount of experience. Didn't you ever wonder why he led this double life? Or why he didn't marry you?'

'I've known other men who didn't offer to marry me.'

'The same kind as him?'

'No, of course not.'

She thought this over.

'Obviously, I did ask myself these questions. At the beginning, as I told you, I thought he was married in the provinces and that his business brought him to Paris several times a year. I wouldn't have been angry at him. It was tempting to have a woman here to take him in and give him a nice home. He hated hotels, I saw that when we travelled the first time. He didn't feel comfortable there, he always seemed to be afraid of something.'

Good Lord!

'Then, because of his character and the way his socks were darned, I concluded that he lived with his mother and that he was embarrassed to admit it to me. More men than you think don't get married because of their mothers and even though they're fifty years old are still like little boys when Mother is around. Maybe that was the case with Honoré.'

'And yet he had to have earned his living.'

'He might have had a little business somewhere.'

'Didn't you ever suspect another kind of activity?'

'What kind of activity?'

She was sincere. There was no way she was play-acting.

'What do you mean? I'm ready for anything now. What did he do?'

'He was a burglar, Mademoiselle Schneider.'

'Him? Honoré?'

She gave a nervous laugh.

'It isn't true, is it?'

'I'm afraid it is. He stole all his life, starting at the age of sixteen, when he was an apprentice locksmith in

Lausanne. He escaped from a reformatory in Switzerland and joined the Foreign Legion.'

'He did mention the Legion when I discovered his tattoo.'

'Did he also mention the fact that he spent two years in prison?'

Her legs gave way beneath her, and she sat down, continuing to listen as if it were another Cuendet, not hers, not Honoré, that she was being told about.

Occasionally, she would shake her head, still incredulous.

'I myself arrested him once, mademoiselle, and since then, he's been through my office several times. He wasn't an ordinary burglar. He didn't have any accomplices, didn't frequent the underworld and led a steady life. From time to time, reading the newspapers or the magazines, he'd hit on a possible target and for weeks he'd observe the comings and goings in that particular house. Eventually, when he felt confident enough, he'd break in and take jewellery and money.'

'No, I can't believe it! It's too incredible!'

'I quite understand your reaction. But you weren't wrong about his mother. Part of the time he didn't spend here, he spent with her, in an apartment in Rue Mouffe-tard, where he also had his things.'

'Does she know?'

'Yes.'

'Has she always known?'

'Yes.'

'And she let him?'

She wasn't indignant, just surprised.

'Is it because of that that he was killed?'

'More than likely.'

'Was it the police?'

She was hardening, becoming colder, less trusting.

'No.'

'Was it the people he . . . he was trying to burgle who killed him?'

'I assume so. Now listen carefully. I'm not the person in charge of the investigation, that's Judge Cajou, the examining magistrate. He entrusted a number of tasks to Inspector Fumel.'

Fumel nodded.

'This morning, the inspector is here unofficially, without a warrant. You had a right not to answer my questions or his. You could have stopped us coming in. And if we happened to search your apartment, we'd be overstepping our authority. Do you understand?'

No. Maigret sensed that she didn't grasp the significance of his words.

'I think so . . .'

'To be more specific, none of what you've told us about Cuendet will be in the inspector's report. It's quite likely that when he discovers your existence and your relationship with Honoré, the examining magistrate will send Fumel or another inspector to see you, this time with a properly issued warrant.'

'What should I do?'

'When that happens, you'll be able to request a lawyer.'

'Why?'

'I said you'll be able to. You're not obliged to do so by law. Apart from his clothes, his books and his pipes, Cuendet may have left some things in your apartment . . .'

The blue eyes at last expressed understanding. Too late, because Mademoiselle Schneider was already murmuring, as if to herself:

'The suitcase . . .'

'It's only natural that, living with you for part of the year, your friend should have entrusted to you a suitcase full of personal effects. It's natural, too, that he left you the key and advised you, for example, to open it if anything should happen to him . . .'

Maigret would have preferred it if Fumel hadn't been there. Becoming aware of that, Fumel adopted a sullen, absent air.

As for Evelyne, she shook her head.

'I don't have the key, but . . .'

'Once again, it doesn't matter. It's not unthinkable that a man like Cuendet might have taken the precaution of drawing up a will in which he entrusted you, after his death, with certain tasks, if only to take care of his mother . . .'

'Is she very old?'

'You'll meet her, since apparently you're the only women in his life.'

'Do you think so?'

She seemed pleased, in spite of everything, and couldn't help letting it show through her smile. When she smiled, she had dimples like a very young girl.

'I don't know what to think any more.'

'When we've left, you'll have plenty of time to think.'

'Tell me, inspector . . .'

She hesitated, suddenly red to the roots of her hair.

'Did he . . . did he ever kill anybody?'

'I can assure you he didn't.'

'Mind you, if you'd said yes, I'd have refused to believe you.'

'I'll add something that's more difficult to explain. It's certain that Cuendet lived partly on the proceeds of his burglaries.'

'He spent so little!'

'Precisely. It's quite possible, likely even, that he felt a need for security, a need to know that he'd built up a nice nest egg for himself. I wouldn't be surprised, though, if in his case another element played an essential role. For weeks, as I told you, he'd observe the life of a house . . .'

'How did he do that?'

'By installing himself in a bistro, where he'd spend hours near the window, or renting a room in a building opposite when he had the chance . . .'

The thought that had already occurred to Maigret now struck Evelyne.

'You think that when I met him at the Régence . . .'

'It's very likely. He didn't wait for the apartments to be unoccupied, for the tenants to be out. On the contrary, he waited for them to come back.'

'Why?'

'A psychologist or psychiatrist would answer that question better than I could. Did he need to feel a sense of danger? I'm not so sure. You see, he didn't just break into a stranger's apartment, but in a way, into people's lives. They were sleeping in their beds and he brushed past them. It was rather as if, as well as taking their jewellery, he took a part of their privacy . . .'

'Anyone would think you don't bear him a grudge.'

Maigret smiled in his turn and merely grunted:

'I don't bear anybody a grudge. Goodbye, mademoiselle. Don't forget what I told you, not a word. Think it over calmly.'

He shook her hand, much to Evelyne's surprise, and Fumel did the same, in a more awkward manner, as if he was troubled.

They were still on the stairs when Fumel exclaimed:

'What an extraordinary woman!'

He would return and hang about the neighbourhood, even when everyone had forgotten Honoré Cuendet. He couldn't help himself. He already had a mistress to deal with who was complicating his life, and now he was going to make sure he complicated it even more.

Outside, the snow was starting to settle on the pavements.

'What shall I do, chief?'

'You must be tired, aren't you? Let's have a drink anyway.'

There were a few customers now in the brasserie, where a travelling salesman was copying addresses from the commercial directory.

'Did you find her?' the barman asked.

'Yes.'

'Nice, isn't she? What can I get you?'

'For me, a toddy.'

'For me, too.'

'Two toddies!'

'Write up your report this afternoon, once you've slept.'

'Should I mention Rue Neuve-Saint-Pierre?'

'Of course, and the Wilton woman who lives opposite the Hôtel Lambert. Cajou will summon you to his office and ask you for details.'

'He'll send me to search Mademoiselle Schneider's apartment.'

'Where, I hope, you won't find anything, just clothes in a suitcase.'

In spite of his admiration for Maigret, Fumel was uncomfortable. He puffed nervously at his cigarette.

'I understood what you were telling her.'

'Honoré's mother told me: "I'm sure my son won't leave me without anything." '

'She told me the same thing.'

'You'll see, Cajou won't want this case to go any further. As soon as he hears about the Wiltons . . .'

Maigret sipped at his toddy, paid the bill and decided to take a taxi back to Quai des Orfèvres.

'Can I drop you anywhere?'

'No. I have a bus that goes directly.'

Was Fumel, fearing perhaps that Evelyne hadn't quite understood, planning to go back and see her?

'By the way, I'm still bothered by that rug business. Keep trying to find out about that.'

And with his hands in his pockets, Maigret headed for the taxi rank on Place Constantin-Pecqueur, from where he could see the windows of Inspector Lognon's apartment.

8.

At Quai des Orfèvres, everyone was exhausted, both the inspectors and the men arrested during the night. The witnesses had been fetched from their homes, and they were everywhere, some barely awake and irritable, pestering Joseph:

'When will they get round to questioning us?'

What could the old clerk reply? He knew no more than they did.

The waiter from the Brasserie Dauphine brought yet another tray of rolls and coffee.

Maigret's first concern, in sitting down in his office, was to call Moers, who was no less busy upstairs in Criminal Records.

They had given the four men's hands the paraffin test. If any one of them had fired a weapon of any kind during the three or four previous days, even if he had taken the precaution of wearing gloves, they would find powder encrusted in the skin.

'Do you have the results?'

'The lab has just brought them.'

'Which of the four?'

'Number three.'

Maigret consulted the list that carried a number against each name. Number three was Roger Stieb, a Czech refugee, who had worked for a time in the same factory on Quai de Javel as Joseph Raison.

'Is the technician categorical?'

'Absolutely.'

'Nothing on the other three?'

'Nothing.'

Stieb was a tall, fair-haired young man who, during the night, had been the most docile of them all and who even now, facing a grilling from Torrence, was looking at the inspector phlegmatically as if he didn't understand a word of French.

Nevertheless, he was the killer of the gang, responsible for covering the assailants' escape.

The other man, Loubières, a thickset, muscular, hirsute fellow, originally from Fécamp, ran a garage in Puteaux. He was married with two children, and a whole team of specialists was now busy searching his establishment.

A search of René Lussac's apartment had yielded nothing, no more than had a search of the lovely Rosalie's villa.

Of all of them, Rosalie was the most argumentative, and Maigret could hear her yelling, even though she was two offices further along the corridor, all alone with Lucas.

They had begun the face-to-face identifications. The two waiters were too overawed to be certain, but thought they recognized Fernand as the customer who had been in the brasserie when the hold-up took place.

'Are you sure you have the whole gang?' they had asked before the identification.

They had been told yes, even though it wasn't true. One accomplice was missing, the one who had driven the car, as to whom they hadn't a single clue.

As was always the case, he would have had to be an exceptional driver, but was probably not a permanent member of the gang.

'Hello? . . . Yes, sir, we're making progress . . . We know who fired the gun: the man named Stieb . . . Yes, of course he denies it. He'll keep denying it. They all will.'

Except for poor Madame Lussac, who was at home looking after her baby with the social worker and who was still in a terrible state.

Maigret was finding it hard to keep his eyes open, and the toddy at the Régence hadn't helped. From time to time he got out the bottle of liqueur brandy he kept in his cupboard for special occasions and took a swig of it, although not without an initial hesitation.

'Hello? . . . Not yet, judge.'

He was being called on two phones simultaneously. It was not until 10.20 that he finally received the call he had been waiting for. It came from Puteaux.

'We found it, chief.'

'All of it?'

'Not a single note missing.'

They had put in the newspapers an announcement that the bank knew the serial numbers of the stolen banknotes. It wasn't true, but the lie had stopped the gang from putting the money into circulation. They had been waiting for the opportunity to offload the notes in the provinces or abroad; Fernand was clever enough to bide his time and stop his men from leaving town while the investigation was at its height.

'Where?'

'In the padding of an old car. Old Mother Loubières, who's quite a strong woman, wouldn't leave us alone.'

'Do you think she's in the know?'

'Yes, I do. We searched every one of the cars. We even had to dismantle them a bit. But we finally hit the jackpot!'

'Don't forget to get a statement from Madame Loubières.'

'I tried, but she refused.'

'Then find witnesses.'

'That's what I've done.'

As far as Maigret was concerned, that was the end of it, or almost. They didn't need him to question the witnesses or proceed with the identifications. That would take hours yet.

After which, each of the inspectors would write his report. And he personally would have a general report to draw up.

'Could you put me through to Prosecutor Dupont d'Hastier?'

And, a moment later:

'They've found the banknotes.'

'The case, too?'

He was asking too much. Why not clear fingerprints as well?

'The case is floating somewhere in the Seine, or was burned in a furnace.'

'Where was the money found?'

'Loubières' garage.'

'What's he saying?'

'Nothing yet. He hasn't been told.'

'Make sure his lawyer is present. I don't want any objections, or any incidents in court later.'

Once the corridors were finally empty, the four men would be taken to the part of the building where the cells were, as would Rosalie – although not to the same room – and there, stark naked, they would be measured and photographed. For at least two of them, it wasn't a new experience.

They would probably spend the night in the cells on the ground floor, because the examining magistrate would want to see them the following morning before locking them up in the Santé.

The case would not go to court for several months, and, in the meantime, other gangs would have time to form, in the same way, for reasons that didn't concern Maigret.

He opened a door, then a second one, and found Lucas sitting at a typewriter, tapping away with two fingers, while Rosalie paced up and down, her fists on her hips.

'So there you are! Are you happy now? You couldn't sleep knowing that Fernand was free, so you found a way to get your hands on him. You're not even ashamed to harass a woman, forgetting that you used to have a drink in my bar and didn't mind me giving you the odd tip-off.'

She was the only one who wasn't sleepy and still had all her energy intact.

'And now you're deliberately humiliating me, putting me in the hands of your smallest inspector. I could eat a man like him for breakfast.'

He didn't reply, but winked at Lucas.

'I'm going to have an hour or two's nap. The money's been found.'

'What?' she screamed.

'Don't leave her alone. Get someone else to keep her company, a big man if she really wants one, and then use my office.'

'All right, chief.'

He had himself driven home in a police car: the courtyard was full of them, given that since the previous night they had been in a state of general mobilization.

'I hope you're going to sleep?' his wife said, making the bed ready. 'What time shall I wake you?'

'Twelve thirty.'

'So early?'

He couldn't face having a bath immediately. He would do it after his sleep. He was just starting to doze off, feeling pleasantly warm, when the phone rang.

He reached out his arm and grunted:

'Yes, this is Maigret.'

'Fumel here, detective chief inspector.'

'Sorry, I was just falling asleep. Where are you?'

'Rue Marbeuf.'

'Go on.'

'I have news. About the rug.'

'Did you find it?'

'No. I doubt it'll ever be found. But it did exist. The petrol pump attendant in Rue Marbeuf is categorical. He last saw it about a week ago.'

'Why did he notice it?'

'Because it's rare to see a rug in a sports car, especially one made of fur.'

'When exactly did he see it last?'

'He can't be sure, but he says it wasn't a long time ago. Then about two or three days ago, when young Wilton came and filled up with petrol, it wasn't there any more.'

'Put that in your report.'

'What do you think is going to happen?'

Maigret, who was in a hurry to finish, merely said:

'Nothing!'

He hung up. He needed sleep. In any case, he was sure he had been right.

Nothing would happen!

He could imagine the starchy look on Judge Cajou's face if he went and told him:

'At about one o'clock on the night of Friday to Saturday, Honoré Cuendet broke into the mansion of Florence Wilton, née Lenoir, in Rue Neuve-Saint-Pierre.'

'How do you know that?'

'Because he'd been keeping an eye on the house for five weeks from a room in the Hôtel Lambert.'

'So, just because a man takes a room in a seedy hotel, you conclude—'

'This isn't just any man we're talking about, this is Honoré Cuendet, who for nearly thirty years . . .'

He would describe Cuendet's method.

'Did you catch him in the act?'

Maigret would be obliged to admit he hadn't.

'Did he have keys to the mansion?'

'No.'

'Any accomplices on the inside?'

'It's very unlikely.'

'And Madame Wilton was at home, along with her servants?'

'Cuendet never broke into empty houses.'

'And you claim that this woman—'

'Not her. Her lover.'

'How do you know she has a lover?'

'Through a prostitute named Olga, who also lives opposite.'

'Did she see them in bed together?'

'She saw his car.'

'And who is this lover?'

'Young Wilton.'

The images in his mind were becoming a little incoherent by this point: Maigret imagined Cajou laughing, which wasn't really in his character.

'You're implying that this woman and her son-in-law . . .'

'We know the father and daughter-in-law did the same thing.'

'What?'

He would tell him the story of Lida, who had been the father's mistress after marrying the son.

Come now! Were such things possible? Could a serious-minded magistrate, belonging to the most respectable classes in Paris, admit for a single moment that . . .

'I hope you have more evidence than that.'

'Yes, sir.'

He had to be asleep and dreaming, because he now saw

himself taking a little package from his pocket and open-ing it to reveal two barely visible threads.

'What's that?'

'Hairs, judge.'

Another indication that it was a dream, could only be a dream: Judge Cajou saying:

'Whose hairs?'

'A wildcat's.'

'Why wild?'

'Because the rug in the car was made of wildcat fur. For once in his long career, Cuendet must have made a noise, knocked something over that raised the alarm, and he was set upon and knocked out. The lovers couldn't call the police without . . .'

Without what? His ideas were no longer very clear. Without Stuart Wilton discovering what was going on, obviously. And Stuart Wilton was providing the money . . .

Neither Florence nor her lover knew this stranger who had burst into their room. Wasn't it a sensible precaution to disfigure him?

He had lost a lot of blood, forcing the couple to clean everything . . .

Then the car . . .

There, too, he had soiled the rug . . .

'You understand, judge . . .'

He would stand there with a sheepish look on his face, holding those two hairs.

'First of all, how do you know they're wildcat hairs?'

'An expert told me.'

'And another expert will come and tear his testimony

to pieces in the witness box by stating that they're hairs from some other animal.'

The judge was right. That was how it would happen. There would be laughter in court.

And the lawyer would flick his sleeves back and say:

'Come now, gentlemen, let's be serious. Is this what their charges are based on? Two hairs?'

Of course, it might happen differently. Maigret could pay Florence Wilton a visit, ask her questions, rummage about the house, interview the servants.

Or, in the silence of his office, he could have a long conversation with young Wilton.

Only, none of that was according to regulations.

'That's enough, Maigret. Forget these fantasies and take those hairs away.'

To be honest, he didn't really care. Hadn't he winked at Fumel earlier?

Would the inspector, with all his unhappy love affairs, have better luck with Evelyne than with the other women?

In any case, the old woman in Rue Mouffetard hadn't been mistaken.

'I know my son. I'm sure he won't leave me without anything.'

How much money was there in the . . .?

Maigret was fast asleep.

They would never know.

OTHER TITLES IN THE SERIES